TO AVOID FAINTING

KEEP REPEATING:

IT'S ONLY A MAGAZINE

. . . ONLY A MAGAZINE

. . . ONLY A MAGAZINE

. . . ONLY A MAGAZINE

. . . ONLY A MAGAZINE

PERPETUAL MOTION MACHINE PUBLISHING
Cibolo, Texas
www.DarkMoonDigest.com

Dark Moon Digest—Issue Forty-One

ISBN-13: 978-1-943720-53-8

PMMP
dark moon

www.darkmoondigest.com
www.patreon.com/pmmpublishing
www.pmmpnews.com
darkmoonhorror@gmail.com

ARTWORK CREDITS
Cover by Trevor Henderson (@slimyswampghost)
Table of Contents Artwork by Allen Koszowski
Interior Artwork by Lori Michelle

DARK MOON DIGEST

ISSUE #41

FICTION

NON-FICTION

Publishers

Max Booth III & Lori Michelle

Editor-in-Chief

Lori Michelle

Managing Editor

Max Booth III

Columnists

George Daniel Lea

Jacob Knight

Jay Wilburn

Founder & Publisher Emeritus

Stan Swanson

DARK MOON DIGEST is published four times a year (January, April, July, and October) by Perpetual Motion Machine Publishing in print format as well as an e magazine version.

All correspondence should be addressed (via e-mail) to the Editor-in-Chief at *DarkMoonHorror@gmail.com*.

Cost per issue for **Dark Moon Digest** is $7.95 for the print edition and $2.99 for the e-publication version which are available in Kindle and Nook formats.

Print editions are available from the publisher at **PerpetualPublishing.com** as well as major online bookstores including Amazon, Barnes & Noble, and many other book dealers. Bulk orders are available through the publisher.

Story submission must be made via Submittable at **https://darkmoon digest.submittable.com/submit** or following the links on our website **www.PerpetualPublishing.com** or blog **www.DarkMoonDigest.com**. Make sure you follow the submission guidelines which can be found on Submittable. Failure to do so could result in your submission being rejected for consideration.

All submissions are read by a minimum of 3 editors, so please allow 90 to 120 days after submitting for response. We encourage simultaneous submissions as we understand the perspective from the writer's side. However, please withdraw your submission if your work is accepted elsewhere. Any submission questions can be directed to the Editor-in-Chief at *DarkMoonHorror@gmail.com*.

THANK YOU TO OUR SUPPORTERS ON PATREON.

Want your name added to this page and saved for eternity? Head on over to www.patreon.com/pmmpublishing and become a patron.

COME CELEBRATE ALL THINGS SPOOKY.

Twitter @GhoulishPod
www.ghoulishpod.com

TEN YEARS OF HORROR

THIS ISSUE MARKS the ten-year anniversary of *Dark Moon Digest*. What an absolutely insane thing to think about. Ten years ago, 2010, I was seventeen and still living with my parents in Indiana. Ten years ago, I hated everything about my life. My family was a trainwreck. If I remained in the Midwest, the only likely future for me was following the lead of my older brothers: abandoning all creative aspirations, having way too many kids, and becoming an alcoholic living in and out of jail begging my mom for money. In 2011, I earned $150 writing Wikipedia articles for indie writers, and bought a bus ticket for Texas. I've never looked back since.

Lori Michelle and I didn't always own *Dark Moon Digest*. We stared as volunteer editors, back when Stan Swanson operated it under his Dark Moon Books imprint. But we certainly fell in love with the magazine early on, inspiring our decision to purchase it from Stan back in 2015. Now *Dark Moon Digest* is published under the indie publishing company Lori and I co-run: Perpetual Motion Machine Publishing (est. 2012). Four times a year, since buying the magazine, we've put out an issue of pure horror magic. I feel very lucky to have a creative partner who is also my life partner. This publishing company, along with *Dark Moon Digest*, is so ingrained in our relationship that it's difficult to imagine life without it.

So, with that said, maybe you can start gaining somewhat of an idea why every new reader means so much to us. Running a magazine is not easy. Especially a fiction magazine. It is tough and depressing and hardly rewarding, but when it *is* rewarding . . . holy crap, it hits hard. I don't see us ever stopping this magazine. If anything, we will only improve by the time we hit another ten years.

A lot has changed since Stan Swanson originally launched *Dark Moon Digest*. I've moved to Texas. Lori's son beat leukemia. We planted a garden. I learned how to blow my nose. We started a YA spinoff of the magazine called *Night Frights*. I took a job I hated and then quit eight years later to make a horror movie (more on that . . . very soon, hopefully). I finally saw *The Thing*. Life is nuts and it only gets more nuts.

I hope you enjoy this issue. A lot of work went into making it, from the writing to the editorial to the design. Thank you for the support. It means everything.

Managing Editor

October 25, 2020

WHEN IT HAPPENS

REBECCA JONES-HOWE

KATE CRINGED AS the emergency room doctor pulled a needle through Michael's wound. His skin swelled against the stitches. Blood and pus oozed through the broken flesh. The doctor dressed the wound in gauze, its white mesh layers covering the bite like a white flag.

Michael's fists clenched when the doctor drew a full dose of the lycanthropy vaccine into a fresh syringe. "It was just a wolf," he protested.

The doctor nodded at the bandage. "It's a precaution, Mr. Freeman. You're better off vaccinated than infected, and our records show that you haven't been—"

"Werewolves don't exist," Michael said.

Kate reached for her husband but Michael swatted her away.

The doctor straightened. "Were you not aware of the reported sighting in the area?"

"I knew," Kate said.

Posters had littered every post along the hiking trail. Everyone else heeded the warnings, but Michael always knew better. Paranoia was control and he refused to give in to it. He'd insisted they go hiking after dinner under the full moon. It was their wedding anniversary, after all. What Kate failed to mention was that her period had just started, and she was sure that the smell of the blood was what drew the wolf near.

"I'm not taking that vaccine," Michael said to the doctor.

"Mr. Freeman, you have to understand—"

"The moon isn't real," Michael insisted. "Werewolves can't exist if the moon isn't real."

"Michael, please don't do this here." Kate met her husband's gaze but his expression only hardened. The vein pulsed in his neck.

"There's proof," he said. "There are videos on the Internet that clearly explain the moon is a hologram."

"I still advise that you take the vaccine," the doctor said. "For the benefit of those around you."

Michael laughed, the maniacal sound drawing attention.

A menstrual cramp worked its ache against Kate's gut. She pursed her lips and gripped at the strap of her purse, the moment's tension swelling against the silver of her wedding ring.

"Mr. Freeman, I can't legally force you to take the vaccine, but I will have to log you down as a carrier if you refuse."

"This is crazy! Either I end up on some government watch-list or you inject me with your mind control drugs?"

Kate caught his elbow but his tendons still flexed against her hold. "Let it go, Michael. You're causing a scene."

"Everyone should be causing a scene!" he shouted, jumping off the bed. "This entire program is a globalist scheme to control us!"

More heads turned. Voices lowered. Patients in the waiting room raised their phones and hit record.

"This is fascism!" Michael roared. "It's blatant fascism and you people are willingly letting it happen!"

Kate gripped at her stomach as the doctor paged for security. She still hadn't gotten herself a tampon and she could feel the trickle of blood working its way out.

***

Kate wasn't going to tell Michael about her period.

He had already gotten his hopes up about her being pregnant this time. They'd been trying for two years already and the only thing that kept Michael from talking about his conspiracy theories was the prospect of them becoming parents.

At home, Kate rushed to the bathroom and popped an extra-strength Tylenol before sliding a tampon in. She washed her hands and returned to the kitchen, where Michael was carefully easing his arm out of his jacket. Kate pulled out the informational pamphlet on lycanthropy from her purse. Listed were the symptoms to watch out for:

Hallucinations.
Hunger.
Stiff limbs.
A need for raw meat.

It seemed surreal, looking at her husband now. The white dressing had soaked up a patch of his blood. The blotchy spot of red looked like an eye on his arm, an outside gaze observing their marriage and the problems it contained.

Michael scoffed at her. "Don't let this government-created bullshit ruin your critical thinking skills, babe."

"I don't want you to turn into a werewolf," Kate said.

Immunization was still the best prevention. The pamphlet said so, but Michael snatched it out of Kate's hold.

"Be serious about this," she said. "What happens if you turn?"

"You're paranoid, babe. The vaccine makes you paranoid. I read on InfoCrusaders that it makes you infertile, too."

Kate shifted. "It doesn't do that, Michael."

"Oh yeah? Maybe you're proof that it does."

Kate tossed her keys down on the counter. She shrugged out of her coat and hung it in the closet before facing him again. "That's not fair."

Michael held his gaze.

"Don't make this about something it's not."

Tendons twitched in his arm. He made a fist, sucked a breath through his teeth. Aggression worked through his gaze, though he looked at her long enough for his anger to ease. His throat bobbed. Wobbled. "Fine," he said. "I'm sorry." He wiped the building streak of sweat off his brow. "I'm not taking that fucking vaccine, though."

"I wish you would," Kate said.

He laughed. "I'll make a believer out of you yet, babe."

***

Michael snored, which kept Kate awake, which kept her staring out at the full moon, its glow slipping over the sheets. She rolled over and touched the edge of her silver wedding band to Michael's arm.

Nothing.

Another snore reverberated against the walls.

Kate took her pillow into the office, but instead of sleeping, she found herself leaning over the computer, where she ended up browsing all the websites Michael had discovered after losing his pipeline surveying job two years before.

InfoCrusaders claimed the threat of werewolves was just a myth perpetuated by the wealthy elite who ran child sex-trafficking rings through rural towns. Occasionally, the mainstream news reported sensationalist stories on child werewolf victims, which InfoCrusaders claimed exposed the truth about the sex-trafficking theory. The larger total of adult werewolf victims, however, were just a part of a false flag operation run by the globalists.

Michael believed that the moon was a symbol upon which the powerful elite could utilize to control the masses out of fear and lore.

He often told Kate that she was a sheep, a follower of the herd mentality.

Wouldn't it be easier to believe it?

Setting up her bed on the futon, Kate lifted the blinds and glanced at the full moon. She squinted at it, trying to see what Michael claimed to.

Satellites all over the world were suspected to project the moon into the sky. Michael swore that the video feed often lapsed. Sometimes lines would blink and flicker. Sometimes the orientation of the satellites would fall out of sync and the moon would appear bigger, smaller, or brighter.

Kate squinted and saw nothing but reality.

***

Part of Kate's job as a public health nurse was to make house calls on new mothers. She knocked on the door of a narrow townhouse and waited for the new mother to answer. Once inside, Kate slipped on a pair of disposable slippers over her shoes and followed the mother's lead up the stairs.

The stairwell walls featured a selection of wedding photos and collage snapshots of a happy couple in love. Already there was a printed photo of the newborn baby in a blue cap.

"This is my husband," the woman said, pointing to the man on the recliner. He cradled the baby over his shoulder.

"We're juggling responsibilities, trying to make it a team thing," the husband said.

Kate set up her scale and smiled, or at least tried to. She weighed and assessed the baby, happy to report that it was gaining weight and thriving. Kate then pulled out the questionnaire she was to ask of all new mothers. Most of the questions were to assess general health and well-being of mother and baby, but there was one lingering question at the end that she hated asking.

"Do you feel safe?"

The mother hesitated. "Safe in what way?"

The question was meant for women who might need assistance leaving abusive relationships. Kate glanced at a living room full of happy smiling photos. A canvas sign hung over the kitchen table that read LIVE, LAUGH, LOVE.

"This question is really about security." Kate shifted against the menstrual cramp that worked against her lower back. "How do you feel about your home and work balance? How do you feel about your ability to provide for your child?"

The husband and wife looked at each other.

"Really good," the mother said. "We're excited. Things are great!"

Kate believed them.

***

The man from the InfoCrusaders website was screaming again.

"People think I'm crazy when I tell them the truth!"

Kate winced before letting herself into the apartment. She tread down the hallway in her shoes, daring to glance at the single wedding picture featured on the beige wall. In it, she and Michael stood posed in front of the waterfall at the end of the Peterson Creek trail, both smiling in their hiking gear, she with a veil and he with a top hat. A budget wedding, but a happy one.

Now five years old, the photo sat crooked in its frame.

"The moon isn't a physical object in the sky, people! It's a mirror they're using to reflect all of their lies about society back to us, and the longer you look, the longer you'll be corrupted. Make sure you arm yourself! Protect your family because I'm telling you now that nobody else will!"

The office door stood open. Michael sat at the desk, reaching into a bag of beef jerky. Kate watched him sink his teeth into the meat.

"They're pulling this trick to try to divert us!"

"Hey babe." He smiled at her while chewing. His gaze lingered. His nostrils flared and Kate shifted in the threshold, wondering if he could smell her now, smell the blood. He paused the video. "How was work?"

"It was fine. How are you feeling?"

He reached into the bag of jerky again, leaning back in the seat instead of pulling out the next slice. "Do I look like a monster yet?"

She pressed her thighs together, hugging at her frame. "No."

"Well, I feel fine," he said. "So you don't need to worry, okay?"

Kate nodded with no choice but to believe, the blood leaking out of her again. The second day was always the worst day. She found solace in the bathroom, washed her stained panties under the cold tap. It'd get better from here, she thought, but nothing could overpower the sound of the man screaming on the computer screen.

"We should be ready! We need to identify our enemy! That's the fight! That's the key! That's everything!"

***

Kate woke to the smell of bacon cooking. She reached across the bed for her husband who wasn't there. Instead, he stood over the stove in his red Visions Electronics shirt. Grease was smeared over the MANAGER title embroidered on the breast pocket. He held a slice of bacon to her mouth. "Take a bite, babe."

The salty cured meat looked as sick and sweaty as he did.

At least it was cooked, she reasoned.

"Did you pack a lunch?" she asked.

Michael laughed. "I'll grab something from the store, babe. I'll be fine. Really." He ate another piece of bacon before pulling his jacket on. He left behind a kiss of grease on her forehead when he said goodbye.

***

Another house, another mother.

Kate counted the children in the photos. Four kids plus the newborn. Kate weighed and measured the baby. She helped the mother get the baby to latch properly. While the baby nursed, Kate pulled out her questionnaire.

This time, the father wasn't in the home, though photos of him were featured prominently. In them, he looked earnest and secure and well-adjusted, with a full beard and a beer gut.

"Do you feel safe?" Kate asked.

The mother nodded. "What do you do if the woman says no?"

"Well, we offer them a card with emergency numbers and counselling options."

"What if you *know* the woman's not okay but she insists she is?"

Kate couldn't help but stare at a picture of the father sitting in the recliner, the two oldest kids in his lap. He was reading *Hey Diddle Diddle* with a smile plastered on his face. Kate couldn't help but wonder if Michael could ever do the same without mentioning the moon wasn't real.

"There's only so far we can intervene," Kate said. "It's tough."

"I can imagine," the mother said. "Gosh, how awful that must be." She glanced down at the baby, bringing it close so she could kiss its little forehead.

***

The moon loomed over the city in its third-quarter waning state.

Kate sat on the deck with a mug of tea clutched to her chest. Chamomile. She hoped it would calm her. Gone were the cramps that accommodated the first days of her period. She'd made herself a salad for dinner, enjoyed a night to herself while Michael worked late.

Her nerves still flared when the sliding door creaked open behind her. Michael placed his hand over her shoulder. Kate took a heavy sip from her mug. She imagined claws forming, hair growing, but when she turned her head all she saw was the moon's glow hitting her husband's face.

"You're trying to see it, aren't you?" His expression was hopeful. Human.

"I'll never see it," she said.

Michael's hand fell from her shoulder. He moved in front of her, blocking the moon entirely. The glow touched his back, his hands, his neck.

Nothing changed.

"Werewolves only change under the full moon, Michael. Studies have shown—"

"Those studies are funded by globalist interests."

"No, they're not," she cried, setting the tea down.

"Said like a true member of the flock," Michael said.

Kate brought her hands to her face. She groaned, pressing fingers to her eyelids until her vision went painful and spotty. For a moment, Michael was a blur, a mess, but it didn't take long for Kate's vision to clear. He still looked like the man she married, still smiled like the man she married.

"What did you have for lunch today?" she asked.

"A vegan burger," he said, "saturated with chemicals."

"Michael, please, just stop. I can't talk to you. You won't let me worry about you."

He sighed, bracing himself over the rail of the deck. "You're scared of me, aren't you? Is that it? You're scared of me now?"

The moon made shadows out of his expression. Michael would insist that they were synthetic shadows.

If they were fake, then how did they manage to cast such menace?

Why, when he stepped forward, did Kate shift back in her chair?

"You think I'm going to hurt you, babe?" He leaned over her and snarled. He bared teeth.

"Stop it."

"*You* got the vaccine," he said, grabbing her shoulders. "It's in your brain now, babe! It's making you paranoid."

Kate twisted in her seat. "Michael, stop. I don't want to talk about this shit." She pressed at his chest and he gripped at her arms in return. He tried to hold on, but his hand slipped when he grazed her silver bracelet. His groan echoed into the night.

"This is why you won't have a fucking baby with me, isn't it?"

Kate wrestled herself out of the chair and scrambled for the sliding door.

"It's been two years, Kate! We've been trying for two fucking years! You're not even concerned!" He lunged forward.

Kate slammed the door over his hand.

***

Kate knelt down in front of him, pressing a bag of frozen peas over the swelling.

"I wasn't trying to scare you," Michael said. "We used to joke. We used to pretend. Remember?"

Of course Kate remembered. They'd turn the lights out and Kate would wander blindfolded through the apartment. It was a game where Michael called to her, played with her. She liked the danger, the strange feeling it stirred inside. Flight or fight. The dread in her stomach always rose up into a lustful rush when he wrestled her down onto the bed or the couch or the floor.

Trying. They had fun trying.

Then the government halted the nearby pipeline expansion and Michael was left with nothing to survey. He spent his nights online, watching videos in his search for something to blame. Every month he'd fade a little more. Stubble lined his jaw. Lines settled over his brow, only to remain there as his skepticism grew.

Secretly, Kate made an appointment to get an IUD.

They tried. They kept trying.

Michael kept tackling Kate down in the dark, recreating the past only to later wonder why a baby never resulted from their effort.

Kate started leaving the curtains open, leaving the lights on.

No more trying. No more thrill.

She was a sheep, after all. Paranoid. Brainwashed.

Michael cradled his hand beneath the bag of frozen peas. The swelling darkened and pulsed. He tried to make a fist, his breath catching, his voice breaking.

"I wasn't trying to scare you," he said.

Kate believed it.

She leaned forward and undid the buttons beneath the collar of his Visions Electronics shirt, her fingertips grazing against the warmth of human skin.

"Let's go to bed, okay?"

***

"I've got a headache," he groaned, gripping at her thighs. When he finished, he rolled off of her, passed out, his mouth gawked, filling the room with snores.

In the night, he rolled in close to spoon her again. He brought his arm around her and clutched his injured palm over her belly.

Kate pressed her elbow against his side in return.

Michael snarled against her ear. "You don't smell like Kate."

She turned to face him. His eyes were wide open, pupils dilated but unfocused.

Kate wrestled herself out of his hold. He growled and reached for her again. Kate scrambled off the bed as Michael thrashed in hallucination, his limbs spasming. His fingers tangled over the sheets.

"Kate!" he cried.

She wedged a chair beneath the doorknob, racing into the office again. Michael's hallucinated calls still penetrated through the wall.

"Kate, where'd you go? What happened to you, Kate?"

A thud sounded. Michael's feet scrambled over the floor. Kate imagined him on all fours, desperate for the smell of her.

He clawed at the wall that separated the rooms.

"We'll fix this, Kate! We'll get it right! Our kids will know the truth! We'll tell them the truth!"

Kate dug through the closet and found one of her old hiking poles, which she clutched tight, poised and ready. Michael kept scratching the wall, his groans turning into sobs, his cries withering into exhaustion as the moon gave way to dawn.

***

The next house Kate visited was a worn post-war home with a rusty chain link fence. In the yard, stacks of undelivered newspapers turned into pulp on the rain-soaked grass. Kate tread up the front steps and knocked on the door.

A dog barked on the other side. A woman yelled.

Kate waited, glancing back at her car as the dog scratched. The woman inside yelled again. She opened the door and held the dog back by its collar. It jumped at her, sniffed at her.

"Sorry," the woman said. "He's just defending the baby."

Kate dodged the dog's swipes as she struggled to pull her disposable slippers over her shoes. Treading across the toy-littered living room, she followed the woman into the baby's nursery. The dog barked behind the nursery door as Kate weighed and measured the baby. She touched the baby's yellowed skin.

"She's got a bit of jaundice," Kate said.

"She'll be fine," the mom said, taking the baby into her arms. "All my kids had jaundice. It went away without issue."

"Jaundice goes away in most cases, yes, but it's worth knowing when to be concerned."

The mother grimaced. Then Kate pulled out the questionnaire.

"You're going to ask about vaccines, aren't you?"

"It is one of the questions, yes."

"I've done my own research, alright? I get that you're a nurse but I'm the parent, here. I'm allowed to make my own informed decisions."

"I have to give you the package with the information. You're free to throw it in the recycling bin just like my husband does."

The mother raised her brow. "Did you vaccinate your kids?"

"I don't have kids. Not yet."

The mother stood, popped the baby on her hip. "But your husband's against vaccines? How would you deal with that?"

"It's something we haven't figured out yet."

The mother laughed. "That's why my husband left me, honestly."

"Was it amicable?"

"Oh, fuck no. He filed for custody. He wants them shot full of chemicals and autism and mind control."

Kate clenched her toes in her disposable slippers, hospital pastel blue, the same colour as the emergency room curtains.

"You'd love my husband," Kate said.

He's turning into a werewolf, she wanted to say.

He'll eat your children, she wanted to say.

Instead, she finished her questionnaire and carefully slipped a vaccination pamphlet between the cushions of the rocking chair. She peeled off the slippers at the door and dropped another pamphlet by the shoe rack. She dropped a stack of pamphlets on top of the decaying newspapers, the dog barking behind her, angry with her, wanting her gone.

***

She found herself at the grocery store, where she loaded up her cart with a salad kit and some saltine crackers and a bottle of white wine. She went down the canned food aisle, where she found Michael with his back turned. He tossed a can of SPAM into his basket.

Kate paused, unsure whether or not to move, but of course, he could sense her now, smell her now. The moon was in its waxing phase now.

Kate gripped the bar of the shopping cart, turning around only to knock over a display of coffee.

"Dammit." She tried to right the display but the bags scattered over the floor.

"What are you doing here?" Michael asked upon his approach. He crouched down to help. The bruise on his hand had healed into a patch of yellow, a smear. His knuckles flexed around the vacuum-sealed packages. He did his best to file them back onto the cardboard shelf of the display, but his fingers seized and the coffee slipped out of his grasp.

"I wanted a salad," Kate said.

Michael struggled to stand. His leg slipped beneath him. Kate offered help but he swatted her back with his curled fingers.

"I'm fine," he said, using the cart to pull himself up. His leg spasmed as he stood.

She thought of the pamphlet, of the warning signs.

"Michael—"

"I'm *fine*, babe."

Another couple entered the aisle. They were young, early 20s, hands still clasped with inexperience. The woman rubbed her free hand over her swollen belly, where a baby was fully-grown, ready to meet the world.

Michael commandeered the cart and placed his basket inside. Beneath the canned meat was a fresh steak. The slab of red pressed against the plastic wrap. Juices settled in the base of the Styrofoam container, sloshing around the white sinews of fat.

A tightness built in Kate's throat. A sickness worked its way up. She squeezed her eyes shut and swallowed.

"Oh please," Michael said, leaning in, his nostrils flared. "I can smell the blood, babe. We both know you're going to be the fucking *Shining* elevator in a couple days."

Kate parted her lips.

Michael fidgeted with the cart. He pushed it against Kate's stomach

"Michael, stop." The alarm in her voice caught the attention of the pregnant woman. Kate put her hand out but Michael shoved her with the cart again. He smiled, tried to make the action playful even though the aggression lingered in his tendons.

"Let's go, babe."

The pregnant woman gaped at them, her gaze brimming with concern.

Kate lifted a hand in acknowledgement, but she still went home with her husband.

***

Michael scratched again at the walls, vigorous, desperate, his voice breaking with need.

Kate moved her camp to the living room. It gave her more distance from Michael and allowed better access to the exit if she needed to run She dug through the dining room hutch for the silver knife they used to cut their wedding cake. She kept it tucked between the couch cushions ready just in case.

Inside, her uterus cramped.

She felt the sickness in her throat.

The moon was nearly full again.

***

She woke to the smell of ground beef in mid-fry.

Michael stood at the stove in his red shirt with his back turned. Kate felt for the knife that she'd hidden. She imagined walking up to him, imagined stabbing him.

Could she?

Michael scratched at the wound on his arm. The bandage was missing now, the wound just scar tissue. The bruise on his hand was missing too.

Like it never happened.

Like everything was normal, even though the beef he loaded onto his plate was streaked with pink and the InfoCrusaders man still yelled from the video playing on Michael's phone.

"If they start quarantining the truth-tellers, then all hell will break loose! This is about individual liberty! Do not let them imprison you for knowing the truth!"

He picked a fork out of the utensil drawer and shovelled the half-cooked meat into his mouth.

"Michael?" Kate called.

The fork slipped out of his hand. He leaned over the plate so he could lick at the juices before returning to the stove for another serving.

"Michael!" Kate stood, the cake knife gripped behind her back.

He fisted the next batch of meat into his mouth. As Kate stepped closer, she noticed the hair growing in the scar tissue of the wound, thick follicles pushing through his flesh.

Finally, he turned, licking his fingers clean. "Oh, I thought I smelt you, babe."

Clutching the knife behind her back, Kate reached for a sheet of paper towel, wiping the grease away from his face.

"I love you," he said, smiling again.

Smiling like in the picture on the hallway wall.

***

Do you feel safe?

She stopped at McDonald's for lunch, got herself another salad.

She ate in the corner, chewing as she watched the television, which featured a breaking story of another werewolf victim found on the Peterson Creek trail.

"I'm terrified," one of the locals said.

"This is horrible," another person said. "There's got to be a better way to deal with this. The government really needs to step things up. I don't understand why they won't quarantine these people!"

A mother cried. "Everyone out there *needs* to get vaccinated. It's the only way to prevent this from happening again."

Kate ate, savouring the acidic taste of her balsamic vinaigrette.

***

At home, a Styrofoam container sat in the sink. The kitchen reeked of raw meat. The smell twisted in her stomach. Her hormones reacted. Her uterus cramped, reminding Kate that her body was a ticking clock ready to spill again. Kate retched into the trash, her eyes closed tight. She imagined Michael's hand on her shoulder, imagined him shoving her into the bed.

He'd find out about the IUD eventually.

In the office, the InfoCrusaders man was yelling again.

"This is the New World Order, people! This is about mass

surveillance! This is about social engineering! They're making us impotent and they're taking our liberty away!"

"Is that you, Kate?" Michael appeared in the office doorway, steak juices dripping off his chin.

Kate wiped the bile off her lips.

"Why don't we eat together anymore?" he asked. Black circled his eyes. "We used to go out every Friday night. Remember that? Remember?"

She could leave, call the police, let them know.

They'd take him for a while. They'd put him into a cell without a window. He wouldn't turn without the moon. Even as a carrier, they couldn't keep him quarantined if he didn't turn.

People wanted a new policy, one that protected the vulnerable instead of the deniers.

"Please," she begged. "Please just get the vaccine."

Michael stared. His gaze hardened. His shoulders broadened. He turned around and slammed the office door behind him.

***

Kate walked up the front steps of another home. She knocked, the colour draining from her face when the once-pregnant woman from the grocery store answered, her swollen belly replaced with a swaddled infant that she clutched against her chest.

Kate put on the flimsy blue slippers and tread over the white shag carpet in the living room. Her fingers shook when she pulled out the scale.

"I was worried," the mother said. "When he hit you with the cart, I—"

It's fine.

I'm okay.

Kate could have said those things, usually said those things. She did her job instead. She smiled like she was supposed to.

"Do you feel safe?"

"Do *you* feel safe?" the mother asked.

Kate thought of the steak, pressed up against the plastic wrap.

"Michael wouldn't hurt me," Kate said. "He seems bad, but he's confused. He's scared."

"Scared of what?"

Kate shook her head. "He's scared of losing me. I know he is."

"Oh, he'll be fine," the mother scoffed. "He'll live."

It wasn't exactly the best answer.

***

Kate returned to an empty apartment.

The garbage had been taken out.

Outside, the moon beamed in its full form. The cramps worsened.

Kate sat down on the couch. She made her makeshift bed and turned on the news. She kept the lights on, the blinds open. The cold hues of the moon's glare competed with the evening's news, where another breaking story flashed on the screen.

Flashing lights. Red and blue. Emergency vehicles surrounded the Visions Electronics parking lot.

A key turned in the door.

Michael entered in his Visions Electronics shirt. Its red shade was deeper now. Blood dripped off the torn fabric. Michael stumbled out of his shoes, leaving a bloody handprint on a door frame, a bloody handprint on the wall. Blood stained his face, his hands, his chest. He looked at Kate and burst into tears.

"I did something bad, babe!"

Kate swallowed, watching as he approached her. He fell to his knees in the moonlight.

"Michael," she said.

He buried his face over her lap. He sobbed over her thighs. "I'm sorry," he said. "I wasn't treating you right."

Kate shook her head, reaching beneath the cushions. "I'm sorry, too."

He gathered a shaking breath. "For what?"

"I don't want to have a baby with you."

Michael raised his head, hurt in his expression. "What?"

She lifted the silver knife.

The stranger in her living room howled out when she struck.

Rebecca Jones-Howe lives in Kamloops, British Columbia. Her work has appeared in PANK, Pulp Modern, and in The New Black *anthology of neo-noir fiction. Her first collection,* Vile Men, *was published in 2015. She blogs about writer life and scathingly reviews V.C. Andrews novels at her website, rebeccajoneshowe.com*

ME, MYSELF

SARAH FANNON

THERE'S A KNOCK at my door and it seems strange that anyone could want something from me on a drenched-cat-Sunday like today. It can't be the postman. Those religious types who go door to door surely would give up and go home rather than hold an umbrella over them with one hand, the other hand steering their bike around puddles. I have no dog for the neighbors to bring to my doorstep after it bit off its chain and got loose in their yard.

When I open the door, I am standing on the doorstep. It is me, wearing clothes I recognize as my own. I'm looking into my eyes that belong to neither my mother nor my father, but some hidden, borrowed genes from dead relatives. I am standing there, looking at myself look at me.

I don't say anything, and neither do I.

I am soaking, and I imagine I want shelter. There is dirt on my arms and my hair. My too-short nails are bloody and ragged, small splinters of wood beneath them. I look down at my own nails, which are finally growing out, rounded and glossy at the top like buttons.

I haven't said a thing. Before I can open my mouth, I close the door and lock it tight, hoping I'll starve and die somewhere. I know if I don't think like that, I might let myself back in. But I can't do that, not with life so light and unburdened. Next time I'll just have to dig the grave deeper.

***

When it's time for bed, I can't sleep. I lay on top of my bedspread and think of myself out there getting washed down the sewer like it's a bathtub drain. I sit up and go down the stairs one step at a time. In the kitchen, I take out a plate and fill it with fat strawberries I know I'll like. The rushing sound of rain gets louder when I open the front door and leave the plate on the welcome mat. It's dark, but I can just make out a silhouette on the edge of the porch that doesn't move. I close the door quickly and slump down to listen, my back against the door.

The front porch creaks and I can picture myself huddled over the fruit, stuffing them into my mouth. When I finally go back to bed and drift into slumber, my last thought is of red juice droplets like little lakes on my skin. I can't remember the last time I was hungry like that. I almost miss it.

***

At work the next day, Nancy barges into my cubicle before I can pretend to be on the phone.

"Your hair looks so lush today," she says. "New shampoo?"

I imagine "detail-oriented" is printed proudly on her resume. "I'm just washing it better these days."

I'm not using new shampoo and I'm not washing my hair any differently. I'm just standing a little taller, a little brighter, a little better. Nancy never used to bother me, but now she stops by throughout the day to soak in whatever it is I'm giving off. She never acknowledges that we've worked together for years and how it was only a few weeks ago she started paying me any mind. She's a moth.

"Well you're practically glowing. Oh to be young again," she says with a sigh, leaning her arms on the edge of my cubicle wall and resting her head on top of them.

I know she said it so I would jump in and assure her that she's not that old. And even though she isn't, I won't take the bait. Instead, I ask how her son is doing. She keeps a photo of him on her desk where he's smiling in his college graduation get-up. It's one of the few things in the office that reminds me I have a pulse. He's got a handsome smile that crinkles his face. He visits the office occasionally and I always burrow away in my cubicle, muttering hello when necessary, his eyes glazing over me politely. But last week, he brought in cake for Nancy's birthday and I marched right up to him to chat and we tossed a spark back and forth like kids playing hot potato. His eyes hadn't glazed at all.

"Sean's doing real well, thank you. Still working on the farm and looking more and more like his father every day."

I refrain from asking if her husband has male pattern baldness. "Would it be inappropriate to ask for Sean's number?"

Nancy claps her hands together in delight. "Of course not! I saw you two hitting it off last week when you met."

She doesn't remember that Sean and I have met before; that I did exist before falling under her radar. I don't even like Nancy, but the reminder that I used to wear my own skin like floral wallpaper hurts.

"He could use a nice night with a nice girl," she says before running to her desk to get a pen.

I don't want to be another nice girl, the kind with a practiced laugh for when something isn't that funny, but wants to be part of the moment;

the kind who doesn't share opinions if it's not beneficial to her; the kind who is so shapeless that "nice" is the only word people can imagine fitting over her head. I've outrun that girl.

Nancy comes back and hands me a paper, and as I tuck it away in my purse, I look over at Sean's grinning photo and grin to myself. If I'd known this is what it felt like to just take what you wanted, I would have done it long ago. I think of all the words I've let wilt away in my chest instead of tasting them. A wasteland.

***

Sean is a slow talker and it makes me hang on to everything he says. We share a bottle of white wine at the restaurant and he pays for the meal, even though I tell him he doesn't have to. He's a real southern gentleman, but not enough to balk at my invitation to come back to my house afterwards.

The porch is empty when I bring him inside and I thank whatever gods are watching over me for that. I politely ask if he needs any water and when he says he doesn't, I lead him towards the couch and straddle him before we've even kissed. His belt makes a thud and clink sound as I toss it to the floor.

"What made you ask my mom for my number?" he asks, holding one of my shirt buttons between his fingers as if he's going to undo it, but in his own time.

"I hope you're not thinking about your mom right now."

"Oh god," he says, and his face crinkles as he laughs, just like in the photo. "Definitely not. I just wondered how I charmed you. You know, so I can use it on other ladies in the future," he adds with a conspiratorial wink.

"Shut up and kiss me."

He does and I can feel it through my whole body. Then he nuzzles his face in the crook of my neck and I hear my porch swing, whining like a greasy wheel. There's only a slight breeze outside, so I assume it isn't the wind. It creaks back and forth, back and forth. I ignore it until it's replaced by a tapping sound against wood, gentle enough to be scarier than brash knocking. Sean pulls back.

"Is someone at your door?"

"I don't think so."

I take his face in my hands, kiss the top of his nose and then his mouth, but the tapping gets more insistent.

"Maybe you should get that," he says.

"I'd rather stay here with you."

"Trust me, I'd love to keep you right here. But it's a little hard to stay focused with that sound."

I begrudgingly get off his lap and open the door. I'm standing there again, looking even worse, like a waterlogged book.

"I don't want you here," I tell myself quietly, and I just blink back. My lips are stained red from the strawberries.

Sean zips up his jeans and walks over. I try to block myself from his view.

"Someone bothering you?"

"No, just a kooky neighbor. Goodnight, Janice," I add and slam the door shut.

When I turn to Sean, there's an unsettled look on his face. Even if he doesn't know what he saw, he knows he saw something lurking in the dark.

"You know, I should probably get going," he says, reaching down to pick up his belt. "Maybe we can get together another time."

"Sure, of course," I say, knowing the chance he'll call is slim. Per usual, I've gotten in my own way.

"Good night."

He gives me a peck on my check, which is encouraging at least, but probably just politeness.

"Let me lead you out."

I see a shadow on the porch swing and I rush him down the stairs to his truck. A hand brushes my arm and I pretend it was him.

After Sean leaves, I bring myself inside. She is weak and no longer recognizable as me. I lead her upstairs and run her a warm bath with strawberry bubbles. She can hardly move without crumpling like origami, so I help her into the tub. She barely ruffles the pink water. I take motherly hands to her head and lather it with shampoo. As I tuck a strand of her hair behind her ear, I can feel bone.

"I have to take you back," I say. "I can't have you orbiting my life."

It feels like her head nods beneath my hands. But maybe that's wishful thinking.

When the water runs cold, I help her out and into a soft, purple towel. I try not to look at her naked body even though it's technically mine. It feels like the least I can do is respect her privacy, especially when her body is concave and wrinkled and shameful.

***

I go farther out this time on roads I don't recognize and end up finding a farm where cows are speckled across the grass. The house is far enough from the land that I don't worry about getting caught. I can just make out the shape of a truck parked in the distance but can't tell the color. I strain my eyes to figure it out but then shake my head, knowing most farmers have trucks.

First, I set the shovel on the other side of the white fence. Then I help her out of the car and put her on my back to climb over the fence. It takes several bumbling tries. The cows barely acknowledge the commotion. I dig a hole and she watches with no emotion on her face. The first time, I put her in a makeshift wooden coffin and she struggled enough that she left scars up and down my arms and I had to wear long-sleeved shirts to work, even in the humidity. This time I'm just leaving her in the earth because I know she's not strong enough to escape.

"I hope you're proud of me," I say softly. "That's all I want."

She doesn't reply. I start throwing clumps of dirt into the hole, my eyes locked on the sleeping cows in the distance just to have something to look at that isn't looking back at me.

***

Sean must have gone to bed and woken up feeling silly for thinking he saw what he did because he calls me for a second date, then a third, until weeks pass and I feel like a new person all over again, the kind of woman who gets to go on enough consecutive dates that she stops counting without realizing when.

One Saturday afternoon Sean calls and asks if I want to join him for a picnic at his family farm. He's never taken me there and I'm oddly excited to see where he spends his days. Sometimes at work I peek over at his photo on Nancy's desk and think of what different jobs we have. I picture him with his eyes squinted, skin glistening in sweat. Now I'll have the proper background, although the scenery is never the point during those daydreams.

He picks me up and I slide into the front seat of his truck with a pecan pie in my lap.

"That looks delicious. Did you make it?"

"I won't even pretend I did. It's time I told you I'm exclusively a grocery store baked goods person. Our kids won't be able to boast that mom makes the best brownies."

Once, my words used to scramble over each other to find the right order, trying each other on for size and drowning any thoughts that might come across too bold. But I'm sitting there, not even worried about his reaction to a joke about children this early. If he doesn't like it, he doesn't like it. I don't have time to step around eggshells anymore, especially not in relationships.

"I don't expect a homemaker. Let me rephrase," he said quickly, "I don't *want* a homemaker. And anyway, that's ideal. Then the kids can boast that their dad makes the best brownies."

We both smile and it almost aches to feel this good. But the champagne buzz doesn't last as the winding roads begin to feel startlingly familiar. I stare out the window for the rest of the ride to distract myself with the blur of green fields and horses and occasional trees. But as we pull up to his farm, I reach out and touch the car dashboard, my breath catching.

"You all right?"

"Yeah, of course."

But suddenly I'm in the dark and smell cow manure and hear a shovel breaking through dirt. Because in a grand slam for irony, his farm is where I buried myself. Buried her, I correct myself. I'm not her anymore.

We lay out a blanket and dig into the food he's packed. It's hard to focus through the picnic until Sean lays his hand on mine and says, "I like you a lot, you know. Even with your grocery store pecan pie."

"I like you a lot too. More than I've liked anyone."

"Really?" He sits up, glowing like a kid at Halloween. "Put a blue ribbon on me."

"Don't let it go to your head, mister."

When he starts speaking, I feel cold breath on my neck. It turns to a whisper: "Weak. Boring. He wouldn't like you if you were still me."

I slap the back of my neck. When Sean looks puzzled, I mutter, "Mosquito."

It barely phases him, and he picks up where he left off, but I can't sit and dish out pleasantries anymore. "I have to show you something. Do you have a shovel?"

"In the shed," he says with a look of confusion. "What do you need that for?"

"Just trust me."

I follow him to the shed and when we get back to our picnic spot, I ake his hand and lead him towards the fence. I hop it and he mirrors ne without question. He lets me work, even takes the shovel for a turn vhen I stop to rest. I don't know what I did to deserve him. Then I look at a scatter of soil tossed over his shoulder and remember I know exactly vhat I did.

"You're worrying me a little here," he says when he hands it back for ny turn. "I'm just praying it's buried treasure."

"Not exactly."

I'm reaching the part where the shovel might rip through her flesh ike its saltwater taffy, so I toss it aside and get down on my knees to hrow dirt out with my hands. But dirt is the only thing I can find.

"She's not here."

Sean steps back. "Who?"

"Me. I'm gone."

"You're scaring me, sweetheart."

Both of us are standing over my empty grave. I turn to read his face and the way he's looking at me, I feel like her for the first time in months. t doesn't matter that I buried her. It was like trying to bury a shadow.

"I just wanted you to see her," I say, sitting down with my legs langling into the hole in the ground. "Maybe you'd like her."

"I think the sunlight and wine have gone to your head."

He doesn't reach to help me up. He just stands and stares at me like 1e has no idea what he's looking at. I imagine her standing behind me, a double exposed photograph, our bodies faded into the outlines of each other.

"I should go."

"I'll drive you home."

Not a word of protest, just a clipped statement and a hand on the small of my back leading us to his car. A hundred threads of excuses run through my head like a filmstrip, but none of them feel right. I know I've blown it and that he's already given up on us, so the more words out of my mouth, the more embarrassing the moment will be for me.

The ride back is silent. I turn on the radio just to have something to focus on and sit awkwardly in syrupy lyrics of a love song, like a punished kid in the corner with cake on her face. When he gets to my house, he idles the car and nods as a form of goodbye. He doesn't walk me to my door like he usually does, when he'll stand on the doormat and cradle my face in his hands just to look at me a little longer. As soon as I shut the door behind me, I hear his car engine whisking away, not giving me a chance to turn back for one last look before he's just a photograph on my coworker's desk again.

I go inside and realize I'm not alone. Never have to be again if I don't want.

We take a bath until our bodies are wrinkled. We sink into the heat and no longer remember our name, if we ever had one.

Sarah Fannon is an honors graduate of George Washington University's English and Creative Writing program. Her work is featured or forthcoming in the LGBTQ+ horror anthology, Black Rainbow, The NoSleep Podcast, *and* SmokeLong Quarterly. *You can find her on Twitter @SarahJFannon and Instagram @ampersarah.*

READ THIS FIRST

BOB DEROSA

I CAN IMAGINE how you're feeling. It must be strange waking up in a random hotel room with no memory of how you got here. You're naked, all your personal belongings gone. And if you look to the right, the first thing you'll see on the nightstand is an envelope with block lettering that says, "Read this first." For the sake of argument, let's assume you did as instructed and upon waking, began reading my letter.

You should know this is no accident. I'm good with computers, so it was fairly easy to hack your work email and figure out your schedule. An investment conference in Houston is a perfect excuse to plan a party such as this. I know you like to drink after a long day of shaking hands and avoiding work, so I assumed you'd end up back here in your hotel bar. And I was right.

It was easy to slip a pill into your drink, and even easier to strike up a conversation once the drug began to take affect. I know you like long dark hair so I wore a wig and crimson lipstick. Even if some of the conventioneers saw us leave, no one would worry. Mainly because they don't like you, but also because leaving a hotel bar with someone you've just met is exactly what they expect of you.

After I walked you to the elevator, I took us up to my room. The room I booked weeks ago. I made sure to get the corner suite on the top floor because that's the floor with all the construction. There's plenty of noise during the day and your nearest neighbor is several doors down. After the drug took full effect and you were unconscious, I put a "do not disturb" sign on the door. I also ripped out the phone line and took your cell phone. On my way out, I sabotaged the door so it won't open from your side. You can bang on the door or wall, but with all this construction, I doubt anyone will hear you. The windows are shatterproof, to ward off accidents or suicide attempts. Which means you're trapped here for seven days. And on the eighth day, when no one checks out, they'll come up and find you. In what state is up to you.

I suppose it's time you take a look at yourself. There's a small hand mirror on the nightstand, next to the butter knife. Look at your reflection. Feel free to scream if you like. If you can. I'll wait here.

How was that? Did you like my work? I made sure to inject a topical painkiller into your face so you wouldn't wake up during the procedure. It was fairly routine. Just a simple cross-stich across your mouth, sewing your lips together. It might have taken only five or six stitches to do the job, but I'm an overachiever so I did twenty. At this point, you're probably trying to scream or at least open your mouth but your lips are tightly closed and that's how they'll stay. For now.

I bet you're going to get thirsty soon. Seven days is a long time to wait for rescue. Maybe you'll figure out how to drink through a mouth that's been sewn shut. But if not, I left you some help. The butter knife.

Look at it now, in all its blunt glory. I bet you would kill for something with a sharp edge. But this is all you've got. You can try and wedge it in between the stitches. Saw at them with that blunt edge. This will probably hurt. A lot. But it's that or die of thirst. It's up to you really. How badly do you want to get out of this? How much do you value your life? I can't answer this. All I can speak to is how much you value the lives of others, which is none. You are a selfish narcissist, but you're also a survivor and I bet you'll come out of this just fine.

Do I hope you'll learn a lesson? I'm not stupid. You need a shred of self-awareness to learn something about yourself and we both know that's not who you are. No, you'll come out of this looking for revenge. You'll try and trace the credit card I used to pay for the room, but that's a dummy account. You'll look at hotel security videos and see a woman who looks nothing like me. And now is when we get to me and why I'm doing this to you.

Don't be mad, but I'm not going to tell you. You'll just have to try and figure it out on your own. I'm sure you'll make a list of every woman you've ever wronged. Every one you've ever hurt by opening that foul mouth of yours and saying the most casual, awful things. This list will be long. And you won't know where to begin. Because I can be anyone. One of your lovers. One of the women at your firm. Your favorite bartender. I could be any of them. And you still have a life to live. So the next time that pretty barista at your local coffee shop hands you a latte, you'll wonder: am I her? Or when you ignore a neighbor in the elevator. Or when a past lover calls you for sex. You won't know. You'll never know.

That's assuming you get out of this. But I have faith in you. They say cockroaches will outlive us in the apocalypse which means the odds are in your favor. Thank you for reading my letter. I wish you seven days of hell. Goodbye.

P.S. I removed all the toilet paper from the bathroom. Just because.

Bob DeRosa's screenwriting credits include Killers, The Air I Breathe, White Collar, 20 Seconds To Live, *and* Video Palace, *the first narrative podcast from SHUDDER. His short fiction has appeared in* Escape Pod *and the Simon & Schuster horror anthology* Video Palace: In Search of the Eyeless Man.

NOW AVAILABLE!
THE GIRL IN THE VIDEO
MICHAEL DAVID WILSON
www.perpetualpublishing.com

The Price of Peaches

ALEXANDRA GRUNBERG

MARY MCFARLANE WOULD have pulled out her left eye for even a bite of a peach.

She plucked the ripe peaches from the branch in front of her, dropping them into the basket at her feet, trying to fight the urge to lick the juice that squished out onto her palm. She would suck her skin dry when she went back to her barrack that night, but Mr. Arthur was keeping an eye on the workers now, and Imogene stood as a fine example of what would happen to those who ate unripe peaches.

"Yer bandage is comin' undone, Dearie," said Imogene, nodding at the wrap that had loosened around Mary's ankle.

Imogene nimbly plucked and placed peaches into her own basket. Mary thought it would be harder to harvest the peaches without any thumbs, but Imogene's basket was already fuller than Mary's, and Mary had all her fingers and thumbs. So far, she had resisted the urge to sneak a bite, and suffer the consequences. She had resisted the urge for the past five days, even though she had not eaten anything since the first morning she came. She could not eat until she got paid, and they would not be paid until the end of the shift. Mary knew from the way the sun slanted down on her neck that the shift was almost over, but her stomach did not seem to know. Her stomach, that craved the reward she would get based on a fully weighted basket, stopped her hand from rebandaging her ankle, where the blister that burst on the way to California never had time to heal. She hoped it would not get infected. But more than that, she hoped she would eat tonight.

"There ain't someone 'round to take care of that fer ye, Dearie?" asked Imogene.

"There was, but he didn't do a very good job taking care of me," said Mary. "In his defense, though, I did a much worse job of taking care of him."

Imogene nodded. Some of the workers here had families, or lovers. Mary and Imogene were two of many who were alone.

A sharp whistle blew, and the workers stopped picking. They rubbed their calves, and their arms, and stretched out their backs. Mary retied the ribbon in her hair, hiding the strands that had fallen into her face. She hated to see those strands. On the journey west from Oklahoma, she thought the dust had settled into her strawberry blond hair, like the unnatural second skin that covered her body, turning it the same shade of dry white. When she reached California, she dipped her hands into the first bucket of water she saw, a dirty trough for pigs that died before she got there, and ran it through her hair, trying to wipe away the dust. But when the dust was gone, her hair was still white, as white as dust, as white as bone. She was thirty-three years old, and she looked as old as Imogene, the mangled crone.

Mary picked up her basket and brought it with the other workers to be weighed. She could not see the number of pounds that Mr. Arthur's assistant wrote down through her bleary, sun-spotted eyes. She could not remember how much money they received per pound, and from what the other workers told her, it did not matter, they would always get less than they expected. Mary did not care how much she got. She would have settled for a penny.

There were baskets of peaches behind Mr. Arthur, and Mary was sure that they were not the peaches from today. The peaches from today ran with juice, and these ones kept their shape perfectly. The prettiest peaches were not the best to eat.

"Listen up, you lousy maggots!" shouted Mr. Arthur, even though everyone was quiet. It was too hot to whisper. It was almost too hot to even breathe.

"Yesterday's peaches, upon inspection, were found to be less than satisfactory!"

Of course they were. The peaches on the side of the orchard they worked yesterday were not ripe yet. They told that to Mr. Arthur, but he insisted that they pick them anyway. There was no juice dried onto her palm to suck off yesterday. Mary wanted to stick her thumb into her mouth now, but she was sure that Mr. Arthur would notice.

"Because they were unsatisfactory, I was unable to sell the peaches," said Mr. Arthur, shaking his head in mock sadness. "Now, what am I supposed to do with unripe, unsold peaches?"

Mary's mouth watered, and she did not know where the moisture came from, but she could just imagine biting into one of those peaches. Sure they were unripe, but she would not mind, nobody would mind. They were all hot. They were all hungry. But Mary could not imagine anyone being hungrier than her. Mr. Arthur seemed like a cruel man, but maybe he thought unripe peaches would be a punishment. It was a punishment Mary would happily accept.

Mr. Arthur took a box of matches out of his pocket, while his assistant poured something over the peaches, something that smelled sour and made Mary gag. Mr. Arthur lit a match, and then set the peaches on fire.

"Let this be a lesson to you, on the consequences of unsatisfactory work," said Mr. Arthur, putting the box of matches back in his pocket. "And in case this isn't enough to get the message through your thick skulls, because I could not sell these peaches, I don't have the money to pay you for today's harvest. If you do a better job, you'll get paid on your next payday."

Mr. Arthur walked away to the big house, followed by his assistant, and the workers, slumped, tired, but no longer surprised by any unkindness, found a familiar clump of other lost souls and started walking back to the barracks.

Mary grabbed Imogene's arm before she could leave.

"When is the next payday?"

"Next week," said Imogene.

Next week. Mary would not last until next week. Her desperation must have shown a shade darker than the desperation of the masses around her, because Imogene did not pull from her grasp, and instead, moved in closer until her lips were by Mary's ear.

"Be careful, Dearie," said Imogene. "There are worse things in the world than Mista Arthur."

She let go and joined the others, while Mary watched the shadows of night run their fingers through the branches of the peach trees. Yes, there were worse things than Mr. Arthur. Hunger was much worse.

***

At night, the orchard looked more sinister, and maybe that was because Mary could not know if Mr. Arthur was back in the house or still watching the peach trees from his perch on top of an old peach crate. She could almost see the shadow of the peach crate, but that was probably because she memorized where it was, just in case she could not resist a lick of the peach juice while she was working. He had not caught her yet, but he caught others, and just the threat of Imogene's hands was enough to make them quake under his verbal lashing.

Mary did not think Mr. Arthur was out tonight, but he told them he had eyes everywhere, at every time, and Mary believed him. She would need to be quiet if she wanted to steal one of the unripe peaches. She thought it was a better spot in the orchard to hunt for food, that the night

watchmen might be guarding the marketable peaches more closely, bu
she still wished she could see more in the darkness. Every branch seemed
like an accusing finger. Every star seemed like a judging eye.

She leaned against the trunk of a tree and felt something like soft fur
brush against her collar bone.

Mary sucked in a shriek, and the brush was gone, and maybe there
was nothing at all, or maybe there was only a rat. If it was a rat, maybe
she could catch it, and eat it. She would happily eat a rat, real meat
instead of an unripe peach. But it was gone. There were only peaches
and when she reached up and grasped one it was as hard as the trunk
she leaned against, but she tugged it off and cradled it against her chest.

When Mary was sixteen, she served peaches and cream at her
birthday party for dessert. She could not finish her plate, and complained
to her father that the cream was too sweet. She had not had cream since
the dust storms first came to cover and tear down her town. The cows
choked in the storms, their lungs filling with dust, and Mary ate the meat
of the dead animals, and there was no more cream. Mary could not
remember how sweet the cream tasted. Now, if given the opportunity,
she would drink the milk raw from a cow's teat, she would drink the
blood out of a cow's neck, but she had not seen a cow, and all she had
was an unripe peach. She brushed the fuzzy skin against her lips.

A branch snapped above her.

There was someone in the tree.

Mary ran, her peach clutched in her hands, and she thought about
Imogene's lack of thumbs, and tried not to think about what it would feel
like if they were cut off. She wondered if she would be allowed to eat
them if there were, but only if she was caught, and she was not going to
be caught. Her feet knew where the root came up to trip her, and even
in the darkness the rows of trees and the paths between them were clear.
And the branch that broke was far behind her now, and the person that
saw her needed to make their way through the darkness, too.

She ran by the pile of burned peach flesh. It was still there as a
warning, and Mr. Arthur liked his warning and would know if it was
disturbed. She did not need burnt peaches anyway, not with one peach
in her hands.

Heavy footsteps splattered through the pile of burnt peaches, and
flecks of peach skin flew through the night air, smacking wetly against
her arms.

He could not have been the person in the tree.

He could not have dropped down from the branches and followed her so quickly.

That could not be breath on the back of her neck.

She considered stopping, turning around, begging Mr. Arthur for forgiveness, but Imogene's missing fingers kept her running, as well as the knowledge that he could not have seen her face in the darkness. As long as she got back to the barrack before him, shut the door and hid under her blankets, she could be any woman who worked for him. He would likely punish all of them for her transgression, but she was too hungry to worry about the others.

A hand gripped her hair, pulling it from its bun with a growl, and her head snapped back as her feet skidded forward. She cried out and her hands flew to her head, and the peach flew to the ground and rolled away into the darkness. One of her hands found the root of her hair, trying to hold it down against the tug. The other hand found flesh, and her fingernails bit in deep, and warm fluid spilled onto her scalp.

A scream cut through the still heat of the night, and the voice did not sound anything like a man, anything like a human.

Her hair was released and Mary fell into the dust while footprints disappeared back into the orchard.

Mary pushed herself to her feet, one hand still massaging her head. She walked into the barrack, closing the door quietly behind her, careful not to wake anyone as she crept back into bed. She found her bandage that once wrapped around her ankle and wiped her hair as well as she could. Mr. Arthur might have seen her face. He might see flecks of his own blood on her dress the next morning. But Mary did not care about that. She could not even think about Mr. Arthur.

All she could think about was the peach that fell out of her hand.

***

"Ye got red on yer collar," said Imogene.

"Maybe I'm sweating blood," said Mary. "Feels like I'm sweating blood."

Was Mr. Arthur looking at her? He might have been. He had a clear view from his perch on the overturned peach crate. His assistant leaned against a tree trunk near him, glasses slipping to the tip of his nose as he ticked little notes on a scrap of paper. He always wore short sleeves, and his arms bore no scratches, though he was far too fat to have kept pace with her last night, anyway. Mr. Arthur was not fat. Mr. Arthur could walk up and down the length of the orchard without breaking a sweat.

Mary tried to wipe off all the blood. Even if it looked like blood, how could Mr. Arthur be sure it was his? Whose else would it be? Would he care if he could prove it or not? She needed the work. But more than that, she needed to get paid. She needed to eat.

"They say a watched pot never boils," said Imogene. "But I'm pretty sure Mista Arthur's always ready to boil over, so maybe stare a little less hard, Dearie."

Mary turned her attention back to the peaches. They did not look as appetizing today. Maybe it was because each handful of peach reminded her of the danger of last night. Or maybe it was because, at this point, a peach would do little to help against the hunger. Maybe it was too late. Mary did not know what 'too late' meant, or how long it would be before 'too late' came suddenly and terribly upon her, but she thought it would be soon. Black spots flashed in her eyes, and her head felt separated from her body, and her stomach seemed to have disappeared altogether. The peach in her hand was like any object, a shoe or a rock, because food was a dream, not something you could hold.

"You're here to pick 'em, not admire 'em."

Mr. Arthur was standing behind her. Mary dropped the peach in her hand into her basket, but he did not move. He leaned against her tree, one hand on the bark, another hand tucked in his pocket. He was smiling, a leering smile, and though a distant part of Mary knew she should be nervous about that smile, it did not hold her attention for long. His sleeves were rolled up to his elbows, and the exposed skin of his hand against the tree was tanned like thick leather. Tan and smooth. Unbroken.

"What've you got in your pocket?" asked Mary.

Mr. Arthur pulled his hand out, revealing it to be empty and just as smooth and unbroken as his other hand, before realizing he should not take orders from a field worker.

"Don't you mind what I got in my pockets, just pick the peaches or I'll find someone else more excited for the work."

Mary went back to picking peaches, and Mr. Arthur stomped away, probably feeling insulted, and probably scheming a way to make Mary pay for it. It was bad, but Mary could not help but smile.

"What's gotten into ye, Dearie?"

It was more a great weight of fear that had lifted out of her like a bubble, carrying the truth with it through her lips.

"I came out last night to eat a peach," said Mary. "I was so sure Mr. Arthur caught me, but it couldn't have been him, I scratched the one who grabbed me, and I was so worried he would fire me, or cut of my thumbs like he did with you, but it wasn't him."

Mary laughed. A few of the workers glanced at her, but kept to their picking.

"Mista Arthur didn't cut off my thumbs."

Imogene was not picking anymore.

"I thought you lost your thumbs because you tried to steal peaches?" asked Mary. "Did his assistant cut them off?"

"I lost my thumbs because I tried to steal peaches, yes," said Imogene. "But it wasn't by anyone who works for Mista Arthur. It keeps to itself, and it keeps to the trees, and it sees more than Arthur will ever see."

Mary had stopped picking now, too, and though they were the only still figures in a sea of sweat and strain, the workers were not glancing at them. They were too focused on their picking now, making too much of an effort not to listen to Imogene, to pretend they could not hear.

"Who was it?"

"Awd Goodie."

"Who?"

"What, Dearie," said Imogene. "'What,' not 'who,' this thing isn't human any more than I'm the Queen of Sheba."

"Then what is it?"

"Hell if I know," said Imogene. "I only know its name, no one's ever seen it, it's too fast for that. Ye just feel it as it runs by, or when it grabs ye, or grabs back the peaches and any fingers that might've been in its way."

"Then you have to eat the peach very fast," said Mary, rubbing her head. "So there's nothing to grab."

"I wouldn't try it, Dearie," said Imogene. "I'm sure if ye eat it, Awd Goodie would grab it back anyway. And that's much worse than losin' a few fingers."

Mary nodded, and plucked another peach, dropping it into her basket. The fruit really was not much. Not enough food at all.

"Is it a ghost, Imogene?"

"Nah, it's flesh and bone. Just no flesh and bone like ye and I have ever seen, or ever wanna see, I imagine. If it gets ye in a corner, it ain't gonna be the wind that comes down on ye, but somethin' much more solid. At least, the teeth that came down on my thumbs were as hard as they were sharp."

The whistle blew, and Mary picked up her basket, carting it over to be weighed. She picked less today than yesterday, but it did not matter. They would not get paid today. Mary did not know if the heat that burned in her head was heatstroke or the beginning of something far worse. But she knew, no matter the danger, she needed to eat tonight or she was going to die.

***

It was dark again, but Mary did not mind the darkness, or the heat, or the faint pain that still throbbed in her scalp, or the blister that had not healed on her ankle. She was concerned that her stomach had shrunk into itself, and yet her body still managed to find a way to be hungry. She forced her body to stay upright as she walked to the orchard, instead of doubling over from the pain of the constant cramps. She forced herself to keep walking until she was far away from the barrack, from anyone else who might get hurt when Awd Goodie came for her, because she was going to get a peach.

She reached up into the branches of a peach tree. The fruit was not quite ripe yet, or else they would have picked it clean this morning, so it took a few tugs to get the peach loose. She did not need to wait long for the response of a thud behind her, as something fell from another tree in the orchard. She should have known that Mr. Arthur could not walk so stealthily in the night. Every step he made was a stomp. Every move he made and word he shouted was an affront to the quiet of the orchard. This thing belonged here, more than him, more than Mary. She hugged the peach to her stomach. It was so small. It was barely a mouthful. It was not enough.

A branch snapped as the creature ran through the darkness towards her, and before she registered the sound there was a sharp pain like a whip striking her arm. She gasped as she fell, and the peach tumbled out of her hand. She cursed to herself, and though she could not see it, she could feel Awd Goodie circling her. Waiting for her to move, but keeping its distance. Waiting for her to give it a reason to attack. She wanted to run. But she was too hungry to be afraid.

Mary reached up for another peach, wrapping her hand around the fruit. The leaves above her rustled, and something wet dripped onto her hand, a thick stream of drool. She froze for a moment, the peach still stuck to the tree, wondering how close its teeth were to her thumb. Then she tugged. This peach was smaller than the last one, harder too, but before Awd Goodie could drop down to her, she shoved it against her lips, biting into the hard flesh and swallowing the bitter fruit.

Her stomach did not want it. Her stomach wanted something softer, more satisfying, and it screamed against the invasion, but not as loudly as Awd Goodie screamed.

Imogene said it would claim any stolen fruit, anyway possible, and Mary expected that when she ate the fruit. So she was not surprised when she was thrust to the ground, the creature on top of her, sharp nails grabbing and tearing the flimsy fabric that covered her stomach. But Awd Goodie was not expecting her to grab back.

Its soft flesh gave way under Mary's nails as easily as it had the night before, like the skin of a peach breaking from the fruit it covered. Mary turned so the creature was trapped beneath her, its blood pooling onto the ground instead of her dress that she would already need to replace as it was quickly turning to tatters. Awd Goodie was smaller than her, and covered with soft fuzz, peach fuzz, but when Mary bit down it was warmer and sweeter than any peach. A part of her knew that in the light, she would not savor devouring this creature, but that part was not her stomach, which enjoyed the blinding darkness almost as much as it enjoyed eating, eating something real, and solid, and satisfying.

In another world, where peaches came with cream, the cries of Awd Goodie would have made her sick. But there were no peaches and cream. There were plain peaches, but even those were denied to her. She would take what she could get, and she would eat, and she would survive.

***

"What are ye gonna get?" asked Imogene.

"A new dress."

Mary held the wad of cash in her hand, ignoring the workers who stared at her sunburned and tanned flesh through the gaping holes in the fabric under her stomach and above her hips.

"Ye ain't gonna have anything left for food," said Imogene.

A new dress would be expensive. But it was necessary. The sunburn on her skin hurt, and she hoped the pain would not become anything serious, but everything could become serious if it just got worse and worse. Dust was not serious on its own, but when it built up and built up it was deadly. Hunger was not serious, until it was, and then it was the only thing that mattered in the world.

Mary would buy a new dress. It was the price she had to pay to survive. And she did not need any food right now. She would not need any food for a while.

Mary was not hungry.

Alexandra Grunberg is a Glasgow based author, poet, screenwriter, and artist. Her work has appeared in the NoSleep Podcast, Daily Science Fiction, Flash Fiction Online, *and more. You can read more of her work at her website alexandragrunberg.weebly.com.*

STEPHEN KING'S SPOOKY ALIENS

STEPHEN KING HAS written two full-length novels that center on extra-terrestrials as the antagonist monsters. *The Tommyknockers* and *Dreamcatcher* have some key similarities in the creatures even with some distinct differences. In both books, they are scary on an existential level and they surprised me in ways I haven't seen in other alien invasion stories. **There will be mild to medium spoilers in this article regarding the nature of the alien species, but not the overall stories or endings themselves.** Proceed at your own risk.

The Tommyknockers in *The Tommyknockers* are not a species in and of themselves, but the result of a parasitic mutation that crosses species through a sort of psychic radiation. The Tommyknockers seed a planet inadvertently and then once "awakened" they set about mutating a new cast of characters into a hybrid version of themselves to go to the next planet.

The process is messy and deadly. New intelligence and new powers develop during the conversion. The intelligence is a barely controlled savant version of intelligence. The mutating subjects behave like meth addicts creating amazing and monstrous inventions with seemingly unlimited power sources and incomprehensible ability. There is a distinct risk of opening a portal inside a star and destroying the whole planet, too.

The Greys in *Dreamcatcher* have phased lifecycles or they are a misbalanced trio of semi-symbiotic lifeforms. You have the classic aliens themselves. You have a fungus that grows and infects species on the invaded planet, but doesn't do so well on Earth. Then, you have a parasitic creature that lives in the intestines to prepare a new species for the assimilation process. In humans, this parasite grows out of control to horrific results.

The commonalities between these species are existential in nature. They are odd and almost backward from what a species that can travel between stars should be. In that way, the revelations about them are unnerving in a way I think most people miss in reading these stories.

The aliens are essentially dumb. They are smarter and more capable than us in many, many ways. That doesn't say much for us, does it? But they are not intelligent enough to understand what they have. They are not builders. They are not progressing as a species. They are spreading like a disease. They use what they find and gather pieces from other places, but they no more understand it than a child riding in a car seat would understand how to build and maintain a car.

Their ships were taken from an older, greater species. The Builders are dead at the hands of these strange parasitic things that are now on Earth. A species far more advanced than us couldn't stand up to these aliens and now the savants are using The Builders' toys to come after us. The aliens in *Dreamcatcher* use more planning and strategy, but the idea is the same. They didn't build their ships and have no idea how to.

There is real terror in the aliens' weakness. The Tommyknockers were the victims in a long string of psychic infections that changed one species and then another until there is no real original species anymore. We'll just be the next victims, and after our world is transformed, we'll board ancient ships we did not build and do not understand in order to seed another world long after we are dead. The aliens in *Dreamcatcher* may not be running the show at all. The fungus may be the real "unthinking intelligence" and they just cart it from world to world to subjugate one species after another to a master with no true consciousness of its own.

Fighting a superior intelligence from the stars and defeating it through our ingenuity to save our planet feels noble and uplifting. It is impossible odds that feel doable with our can-do spirit. Facing something that lives by altering our own intelligence or fighting omething superior to us that may have no identity at all, feels alien in a osmic horror sense. These are not simply people in alien form we can eason with or defeat like any other army on Earth. This is a creeping, ubversive, unfathomable force that attacks us the way diseases, ddiction, or mental illness attack our identities and our sense of self.

It is the small, flawed, stupid, base nature of King's two forms of alien nvaders that make them truly alien and truly unnerving. Perhaps not oy coincidence, both novels involve the town of Derry and references to he It, that creature who should be dead. That malignant intelligence was lso of extraterrestrial origin and leaned heavy into cosmic horror. When 5tephen King decided to invade from space in his novels, he chose to nvade our sense of self by undercutting our expectations of spacefaring liens and making the invasions personal to our identities, not just a imple threat to our civilization or governments.

ay Wilburn taught elementary and middle school for 16 years. He has two sons. 4e's the author of the Time Travel Academy *series for middle grades readers,* Lake 5catter Wood Tales *for middle grades and younger readers, and the* Maidens of 'ombie Kingdom *trilogy for young adults.*

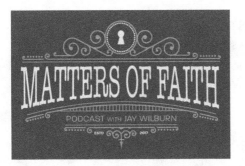

In Our Town, Everyone's a Writer

ANDY DAVIDSON

HE OWNED OUR little bookstore. Was also the mayor. We all knew he was a cokehead. Had that Jitney Jungle coffee can on his desk in a closet office upstairs, over by POETRY and CREATIVE NONFICTION. Said it was the receptacle of the ashes of our treasured autodidact whose prose had only ever met with obscurity and a few good bar stories among the college set. He'd labeled it with a yellow Post-It Note: "Don't Touch—Here Lies Tommy." We knew Tommy—a sad sack who wrote poems and sold T-shirts to tourists and started up a juice bar went bust. He's hit by a pickup on the side of the road late one night, walking home drunk from Smokey's. What come of his ashes, who knows. But it weren't no Tommy in that can. Our mayor was a liar. We knew that, too.

We knew bout the parties at his house up on the hill, just down from that other manse, one where our famous writer had lived half a century before. Some called it weird sacrilege—hedonistic cocaine orgies a block from the backyard grave of a literary genius who'd supposedly died whilst scribbling on plaster walls in his own goddamned blood (a wall-sized paragraph of gibberish, no punctuation). But it weren't like that, it was no intended desecration. They was just the mayor and his habit and we figured it was all part of some great and secret history we was privy to. Our own dirty little mythology.

But they was things we didn't know.

About the room in the mayor's basement.

What his wife prayed to down there.

Rich people and hypocrites and liars, that's what I say. Spit on em and the devils they worship, I'll have no part of it.

Still: I never laughed at another man's dreams. Nor his troubles.

Some will. I won't.

Our mayor, boy, he had em though. Dreams and troubles.

***

A girl went missing out at the lake, one week before the cops broke open the front door and forced the mayor down on his belly, naked and kicking and spitting. She's a part-time student. Also, a hostess at the Golden Palace—not the old one, but that new one they rebuilt over by the Walmark? I only tell it cause I remembered her, when I saw her picture in the paper. She'd served me up takeout lemon pepper chicken and rice and give me extra sweet-n-sour, didn't charge me for it, even though the sign clearly said it was policy on the register: "They is a charge for extra sauce." She had a nice smile. One eye sort of pulled in toward the other, like she was out of true. Last person seen her alive was her boyfriend. It were a gray Saturday and they'd gone out to swim at the little freshwater beach, only they couldn't on account of the wind had blown in about a thousand seabirds from the coast, and the water was full of them like they was having a convention. Boyfriend went over to the park bathroom to relieve himself, left her sitting on a towel in her bathing suit, looking out at them terns and pelicans. I believe they was gulls, too. I can see her now: one hand cocked over her eyes when the sun cracked the clouds, hair blowing round her face. He come out of the can, she was gone. Her towel'd blown off and snagged on the leg of a SWIM AT YOUR OWN RISK sign. I don't know why, but I picture it a red towel.

***

Far as the mayor's troubles went, none of us figured how broke he was. He'd long talked up turning our town into what he called a "destination for writers": getaway cabins down by the creek that ran through the greenest part of the city, literary-themed packages at a new spa off the square, meant for the East Coast elite. Little pink houses on the bypass you could rent and finish that series bible. Less a destination, more a theme park, you ask me. On the other hand, as y'all know, we are not strangers to eccentricity here. Hell, I've heard worse dreams. After all, we did have us a world famous writer and a bookstore. Also had the college, where professors of English brought in guest poets for the big bucks. It only made sense our mayor'd try and capitalize on it. Though maybe we should of known something was loose, I mean, he did file Stephen King with the science fiction. Anyone ever read a book knows better than that.

Anyway, it all came out, after the raid. It was a series of stories made the state *Gazette*. Because of the kidnapping charges they'd brought in the FBI and the FBI went through that house with a fine-toothed comb and they found secret ledgers in wall safes and all sorts of incriminating records on the mayor's home computer. Fraud, tax evasion. You never suspected. They found other shit, too. Internet print-outs of naked children committing vulgar acts upon one another. Secret black mass how-to rituals to summon Satan.

Then there's the basement. That was a whole nother thing.

We found it all out from this old boy worked for the sheriff's department, was first on the scene. He used to come out to the spillway and fish with us on a Sunday. As it happened, I don't know why, he and I was the only ones out there a few weeks after it all went down. We hadn't neither of us caught a goddamned thing and I was fixing to haul in and head for the bar where it was rumored Old Smokey'd gone and got himself a nutria and was billing it as The Giant Rat, as in "See The Giant Rat—One Dollar." But then this boy, he just opened up and started talking like that water pouring out from the dam, and he told me and I'll tell you and then we'll all know it.

Said he was third through the door.

Said them other two broke upstairs and the Feds came in after him and tackled our mayor in the living room, who was buck naked and smeared in blood and scrabbling for a shotgun in a glass case, had punched right through the glass, high as Old Rocky Top. Deputy, he followed sounds down them stairs, he said, walls aglow with a honey light: chanting, in a hoarse voice, spewing all manner of nonsense and babble. That voice was shredded, like she'd been at it for days. Maybe she had. "You couldn't even tell it was a she," he said. But he got to the bottom and saw it was: the mayor's wife, prostrate and naked on the Travertine, and she's a screaming and a hollering and invoking the names of deities black and strange. All around her candles and the smell of her own shit and her face in this thick bastard of an old weird book, a book without words save the ones she herself was scribbling with a pen dipped in a metal coffee can. And after each line set down she'd cry out whatever nonsense was scratched there, and then, he said, she'd *lick it* clean off the page. "Lick it," he said, and spat snuff into the water and moved his cork a ways. And them pages? "They was writ in blood," he said.

Six feet away, hanging from the floor joists by nylon rope, was that college girl. Only a few scraps of clothes left on. Bite marks the Feds would later match up to the mayor's mouth. Weren't the bites that killed her, though. The papers told that. It was the cuts. Here, there, like a hundred little eyes had cracked opened on her and started weeping red (my words, not the paper's).

The mayor's wife, she never even saw that deputy there. He'd slunk back against the wall. Said he was crying by the time the Feds got down.

I don't believe either of us caught anything that day.

***

Among the other things we'd always known: the mayor's wife had literary aspirations. She was part owner of our bookstore and the two of them had brung in a parade of literary types over the years—not just writers but they agents and editors. Wined and dined them all until one of them agreed, I suppose, to look at that novel she had. It did not go well. Some even said it was this misery that led to the mayor's cocaine use. Rich people, I say, and the devils they worship.

But it did make me remember that famous writer and his wall of gibberish. So I went out one day and took the tour. Let the little English major with the pink bow in her blonde hair tell me all about the story behind that wall. She had a twinkle about her, I'll give her that. Something mischievous beneath her docent's smile, like she didn't buy it no more than I did. How the wall would of been the start of his last great masterwork, a book written in the language of an alien race or some such shit. Had he only lived to finish it, had the alcohol not pickled his brain. All I could think of was what that deputy had told me: how the mayor's wife had licked those pages clean.

I pointed up to the top where the plaster met the cornice and the gibberish began. Letters big and crooked and childlike and signifying nothing. It had a ladder against it. "What's happening up there?" I wanted that girl to tell me.

She said, "Water damage?" and smiled.

I felt something then, some pang I had not felt in a long, long time, like the creak of an old house in the night, pushing against its frame.

Then she laughed and I seen her tongue all red, and I shivered.

***

We moved on, elected ourselves a new mayor. Chalked it up to a history more secret than even we knew, as folks do, in towns like ours, when some long-unturned stone gets kicked over. Bad things ain't so uncommon you can't reason em out: money problems, literary rejection. Alcoholism. Insanity. We tell ourselves stories as much as we tell them to others, don't we? In our town, everyone's a writer.

One thing nipped at me, though, ever time I passed that shuttered bookstore, usually headed around the corner to Smokey's, where you could trust not to be swamped with sorority gals on a Tuesday afternoon (that nutria was already dead; he'd fed it lettuce in a wire cage and it just went to sleep one day and did not wake up, dreaming, I suppose, of duckweed and brown water). It weren't a big thing, but it felt big, somehow. A piece of some puzzle we'd all missed. Or I'd missed. A puzzle of what, though? I don't know. Maybe I figured if it wasn't Tommy's ashes up there in that can, and it was still there, well, a few bags full of dope might see me through some old debts paid. Keep me out of new ones. We all want better things than we generally have. Maybe that was it. Maybe it was that simple.

I got in through the back, an elbow to a pane of glass in the alley.

They could of been an alarm. If it was, it was silent. It made no difference, in the end. I moved through the dark and went up the stairs and came out the second floor landing where they had this big thousand-dollar bust of our town's famous writer, and he had a solemn, sober face, owllike in its wisdom. "Aw, lick it," I said to him, and kicked open that little closet office next to POETRY, and there it were, sure as Sunday Meeting: nestled in among the pens and scraps of paper and half a dozen stacks of advanced readers' copies of books that sumbitch would never read or sell, the Jitney Jungle coffee can.

I recalled what that deputy said, how the mayor's wife had dipped that poor girl's blood out of a coffee can. He didn't say what kind of can. The papers, not a one, ever said a thing about no coffee can. Nothing about no book neither. Like he'd made it up or it weren't there by the time them Feds got downstairs.

I reached out and yanked off that little Post-It Note and crumpled it.

It were an old tin, sealed with a new plastic Tupperware lid the mayor had managed to jam on. I peeled it back and looked inside.

It weren't Tommy.

It weren't the dope we thought it was.

It were something else. Something beautiful.

A deep, dark, glittering emptiness, welling up red.

It were us.

For Barry Hannah

Andy Davidson is the Bram Stoker Award-nominated author of In the Valley of the Sun *and, most recently,* The Boatman's Daughter. *He lives in Georgia with his wife and a bunch of cats.*

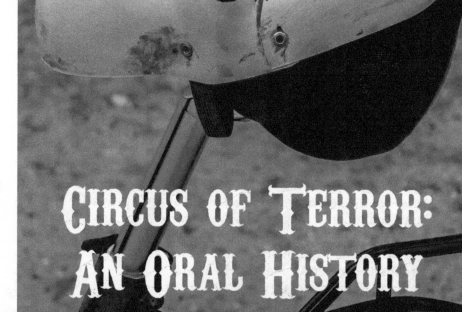

CIRCUS OF TERROR:
AN ORAL HISTORY

TRAVIS KENNEDY

CELEBRATING THE TEN YEAR ANNIVERSARY OF THE SMASH HIT FILM, *YEAR OF THE CLOWNS.*
CLASSICS REVIEW MAGAZINE, OCTOBER 9, 2029

IT'S HARD TO believe that it's been ten years since the found-footage classic *Year of the Clowns* crash-landed in theaters like a supernova, forever changing the way that independent filmmakers found audiences online and exposing the world to a trio of talented artists who redefined the limits of guerrilla horror production. The homemade film—captured entirely on personal devices by its stars—became a sensation for its startlingly realistic special effects (on a non-existent budget), and for the filmmakers' steadfast commitment to the hoax—even today.

To celebrate the anniversary of *Year of the Clowns*, Classics Review secured rare interviews with the filmmakers themselves,* alongside witnesses, experts, and the studio that turned this homemade thriller into a global sensation.

With no further ado, we're thrilled to take you back to the Maine woods, circa 2016: *The Year of the Clowns.*

Classics Review was unable to track down the film's breakout lead, Lucas Jarrett, despite an exhaustive search. His name still appears on the Federal Registry of Missing Persons.

PART I

"You couldn't find a clown costume anywhere. They were all sold out."

In the fall of 2016, an independent film crew staged sightings of a creepy-looking clown lurking in a parking lot in Green Bay, Wisconsin as part of a marketing campaign for their short film, "Gags." The footage earned national news coverage, and it almost instantly spawned the "2016 Clown Sightings" trend across the United States. Copycats disguised as "evil clowns" started popping up alongside highways and at the edge of the woods in dozens of cities and towns from Florida to Washington and everywhere in between. Over the course of several weeks, clowns made appearances in every state in the country.

In the small, suburban town of Hunter's Ridge, Maine, three young filmmakers set out to capitalize on the phenomenon.

SEAN DUNTON, *Director/writer/"Sean"*:
We weren't filmmakers. We were just kids, horsing around.

JASON BELANGER, *Director/writer/"Jason"*:
We were bored, and we wanted to go viral.

DUNTON:
I mean, we hoped our video would catch on, but we didn't put that much thought into it. I know that isn't what you want to hear, but it's the truth.

BELANGER:
I was home from college. Sean, too. Lucas didn't go to college.

DUNTON:
Lucas was working at the gas station. And he had a side business.

BELANGER:
He was selling weed.

DUNTON:
Everything is so different now. It was still illegal then, so you had to know a dealer. And if you wanted to buy pot, you kind of had to hang out with the guy who sold it to you.

BELANGER:
Honestly, I don't know if we would have called him otherwise. We were going in different directions by then.

DUNTON:
I hadn't talked to Lucas since summer, but Jason kept in touch with him a little. Enough to know he was dealing, anyway. We had two days in Hunter's Ridge with nothing to do, so we wanted to score some pot and go to the movies. We went to Lucas's apartment downtown, above the thrift shop. He moved there after his dad tossed him out.

BELANGER:
He told us he left home on his own, but who knows with Lucas. He was in kind of a dark place.

DUNTON:
He was obsessed—and I mean, *obsessed*—with those clown videos.

BELANGER:
He had a huge TV. Like 75 inches, mounted on the wall in a crappy little apartment with holes in the ceiling and no food in the fridge. He would just sit there casting his phone to the TV, making us watch the clown videos.

DUNTON:
Don't get me wrong, we thought they were funny, too. But there were hundreds, man. Some of them were videos, other ones were just pictures. And Lucas couldn't get enough. I've never seen him more focused on anything in his life.

BELANGER:
He really wanted to do it.

DUNTON:
We all did. We were dumb 20 year-olds, and we got talking about doing a clown vid. We thought it would be funny.

BELANGER:
We were also just, *blazing* high.

DUNTON:
So we were feeling extra creative, in the moment. And we got talking about how we could make sure our video went viral.

BELANGER:
The clown thing, by then, was already getting kind of played out. Everyone was doing it. If you wanted to stand out, you had to come up with something new.

DUNTON:
Me and Jason got talking about how nobody was telling it from the clown's perspective, and how crazy it would be if we were like, freaking people out and getting their reactions while *they* were trying to take videos of *us*.

BELANGER:
I say again, we were really stoned. Sean had just taken this film class I guess, and he couldn't shut up about perspective and line of sight.

DUNTON:
Yes. I took a film class in college. It's one of the things people always point back to when they say we faked the footage. As if one semester in "elements of film production" could teach me how to do *that*.

BELANGER:
Lucas was getting pissed.

DUNTON:
He hated how much we were focused on recording. I don't think he wanted us to film it at all.

BELANGER:
Lucas just wanted to screw with people and break stuff.

DUNTON:
Lucas was one of those guys, you were always stressed out going somewhere with him because you knew he was probably going to get in a fight.

BELANGER:

He was always a little aggressive, but by the time we graduated it was getting pretty tough to deal with.

DUNTON:

.t's hard. When we were in third grade I was the runt in class, and I got picked on a lot. Lucas would stick up for me. I always thought he was a hero. But he went from keeping me out of fights to dragging me into them. And he would always bring up third grade if I didn't, you know, "have his back." It got worse in high school. We thought there were problems at home, maybe.

BELANGER:

I'm pretty sure his dad beat him up.

DUNTON:

Anyway. We went to the costume store, and they were all out of adult clown costumes. Everyone was trying to be in the next viral video.

BELANGER:

You couldn't find a clown costume anywhere. They were all sold out. We drove around for an hour.

DUNTON:

So we were over it pretty much right away. Jason and me, I mean.

BELANGER:

I kind of thought it was proof that the whole thing had jumped the shark. But Lucas insisted. He said we should just make our own costumes. We agreed to go back to our houses and see what we could put together, then meet at Lucas's place.

DUNTON:

Jason and I were going to bail at that point. I wish we had. He would probably have written us off for good. Maybe kicked my ass later. But he would still be alive.

BELANGER:

I don't want to get into that question. Yes. He's dead. Or, *Lucas* is gone, anyway. I'm not going to litigate it. So we talked about it, and we felt kind of guilty, like we were taking advantage of him for the pot if we ghosted. And we figured it was worth trying if we could get some good footage. It's the biggest regret of my life.

The first shot of the film is Jason, emerging from the bathroom a Lucas's apartment in full costume. He is wearing a pair of tangerine colored pants and a bright green dress shirt. His face is painted white and he's wearing a rainbow-colored afro wig. Once the boys stop laughing at him, we see Jason affix the headband with a HeadCam recording device to his forehead, and adjust the frizzy hair of the wig around the lens to keep it concealed. The perspective changes to Jason's view then, a shot of Sean and Lucas sitting on the couch in hysterics.

PETE SILVER, *editor:*

Sunrise Studios brought me on to edit the footage after they bought it from the guys. I love that transition—switching to "Clown's Eye View." It really puts you in the middle of it. And Jason's costume was just so funny.

BELANGER:

It wasn't very intimidating.

DUNTON:

My costume looked basically the same as Jay's, except I had a tie-dyed tee shirt. And just jeans, I didn't have those electric pants that he found in his dad's closet. Same wig and makeup, though. We got them at the hardware store. Lucas's costume was a whole different story.

BELANGER:

You can see the camera shake a little when he first comes out of the bathroom. That was me shuddering. He had obviously been planning this for a while.

Lucas's mask is lumpy and shock white, with large black circles for eyes and bushy tufts of gray hair over the ears. The nose is long and crooked, and the mouth hangs slightly ajar, showing off a mishmash of long, jagged teeth. Black face paint around the mouth forms a menacing, crooked smile. He is wearing a ratty, dark gray three-piece suit from the Salvation Army and combat boots, and he looks like he would fit right in among the abominations in a depression-era freak show. The final piece is the gloves: they're snug fitting with long, gnarled, rubbery white fingers and black fingernails. He had taken them from an expensive vampire costume.

BELANGER:

We have no idea where he got that mask. I mean obviously he stole it, but we don't know from where.

DUNTON:

You've seen it. The mask was terrifying.

BELANGER:

The knife is what really freaked me out, though.

Lucas wore a holster, the kind Crocodile Dundee might sport, and sticking out of the leather pouch was the handle of a very long—and very real—kitchen knife.

DUNTON:

We knew the knife was trouble. If Lucas is going out hellraising and he has a knife on him, he's gonna find a reason to use it.

BELANGER:

At the very least, he was gonna chuck it at a squirrel.

DUNTON:

So we got everything recording and streaming, and out we went.

GARY PINCIOTTI, *Executive Producer, Sunrise Studios:*

That shot of Lucas and Sean walking up the hill toward the setting sun was what sold it for me. It was found footage quality, but with style elements lifted right out of classic westerns and horror films. I knew right away, those kids knew their stuff.

BELANGER:
I had forgotten my HeadCam was even recording by then.

PART II

"We felt like we had the market cornered on the whole 'evil clown' thing."

The boys' planned to spend a few hours hiding in conspicuous places, to catch the unsuspecting townsfolk of Hunter's Ridge off-guard. They wanted to interact with people directly, jumping out from behind buildings and chasing school buses. They planned to piece together a simple narrative for their characters later, and splice it in between the footage of them terrorizing the town.

The narrative would be loosely based on the real Hunter's Ridge legend of the Stupendous Freaks.

BELANGER:
I guess it was gonna be kind of *Borat* style. You know, mess with people in real life and then fill the story in after?

DUNTON:
God, we were pricks.

BELANGER:
We figured we had the Stupendous Freaks, which would make for a good jumping off point. Everyone in Hunter's Ridge knows about the Freaks.

The next fifteen minutes of the film are a dramatic recreation of the history of the Stupendous Freaks Carnival. This portion was created by Sunrise Studios.

DUNTON:
There were these actual psychopaths who dressed like clowns in Hunter's Ridge in the 1930s.

BELANGER:
Circus freaks. I think it was the 1800s.

DUNTON:
We felt like we had the market cornered on the whole 'evil clown'
thing. I mean, this stuff really happened.

HERMAN FINCH, *Proprietor, Hunter's Ridge Historical
Society:*
There's no printed record of the legend itself, but photos of the
"Stupendous Freaks Carnival" in Hunter's Ridge are dated September,
1927. The story goes like this: a traveling carnival came to town that
autumn. Back in those days carnivals were often regional acts' -. Think
of the Ray Bradbury book. They didn't call ahead and get a license,
they didn't have insurance. Oftentimes they weren't much better than
organized thieves and con artists, who would piece together little
carnival acts as a grift to rob a town blind. The Stupendous Freaks
were among the worst.

The workers all dressed identically—as clowns—for their entire stay,
and we think the reason was so that nobody could be identified. So the
carnival set up in town, and started drawing complaints right away.
People were getting injured on the rides. Losing valuable items in the
funhouse. There were burglaries throughout the village. The clowns
were rude and intimidating, and they were handing out really
disturbing materials to the children—devil worship stuff, photographs
of nude women in giant masks, performing graphic sex acts. And so
on. The pieces featured in the film were genuine. We have some of it at
the Society.

It all came to a head on the fifth night. A high school girl was assaulted
behind the schoolhouse. Absolutely horrible. The carnival wouldn't
turn over the perpetrators, and since they were all dressed alike the
girl couldn't identify them. They started to pack up to leave instead. It
became an angry mob scene. The townsfolk burned down their
wagons, destroyed their sets. And they chased the clowns off, into the
forest.

A few years later, people started claiming that they spotted clowns at the edge of the woods, watching them. The clowns never left the trees. They just stood there, watchingMen set out into the woods, worried they might come across a band of vengeful, devil-worshiping clowns living outside Hunter's Ridge, but they never found anything.

Every few years since then, someone will see a clown in the woods. And as I'm sure you know, disappearances outside Hunter's Ridge are more common than anywhere else in the state. Hunters, tourists, children occasionally, have been known to wander into the woods and never come back. These vanishings usually occur shortly before or after a clown sighting.

Or so the legend goes.

Nearly an hour of screen-time is spent on the boys raising hell around Hunter's Ridge. There are no horror elements in the footage, although Sunrise Studios added a subtle, haunting score and handheld shots of actors portraying the boys, filmed from a distance like someone watching them from the forest—as if they're being followed. It's well done, and very much an homage to the original Halloween. *But then again, most horror movies are.*

DUNTON:
We were just being stupid. Jay chased a school bus, but he looked so ridiculous that the kids were laughing at him. We saw half a dozen cellphones taping though, and that was the goal. Lucas lingered around the parking lot of the Quick-Save, way too close to people getting in their cars. And he screamed in the boxes at drive-throughs.

At one point a car pulls up while we're walking down the road, right? And we're all thinking it's gonna be the police. But when we looked over, it was this old Chevy and there were four kids dressed like clowns in it. They were doing the same thing we were.

BELANGER:
One of the kids in the back was filming. The kid in the passenger seat flicked a cigarette at us and they peeled out.

DUNTON:

God, did that make Lucas mad. He wanted to get his car, track 'em down.

BELANGER:

I didn't like how he kept pulling the knife out of his holster every few minutes after that.

DUNTON:

It was when we went through the Quick-Save that things got out of control.

BELANGER:

He went first, and we were right behind him. Lucas's version of "freaking everyone out" was pulling stuff off the shelves, tipping over a sunglasses display, screaming in the clerk's face, stealing a bag of beef jerky.

DUNTON:

He didn't even eat it.

BELANGER:

Me and Sean didn't touch a thing. We didn't say a thing. Remember, we didn't have masks on like him. We were seriously worried about getting in trouble, and we felt kind of bad about it, too.

DUNTON:

That poor clerk didn't deserve Lucas.

BELANGER:

Like, do they kick you out of college if you get arrested?

PART III

"This is real. You have to believe me."

As Lucas's behavior continues to spiral, the boys find their way toward the edge of the woods. Drone shots added by Sunrise establish the wide expanse of trees just beyond the roads they're traveling.

DUNTON:

The Quick-Save really got Lucas going. He was just disturbing-the-peace now.

BELANGER:

He threw a rock at the windshield of a Kia. Lucky he didn't cause a car accident. He started banging on people's doors, pounding on windows.

DUNTON:

He chased three kids on bikes, waving his knife around. A little girl fell off her bike and I swear, I thought he was gonna hit her.

BELANGER:

You see it in the movie. We ran out there and I held Lucas back while Sean got her on her feet and told her we were sorry. Honestly, I can't believe I put my hands on him.

DUNTON:

It was pretty brave of Jay.

PETE SILVER, *Editor*:

We had to make a lot of judgment calls about what we could leave in and what we should take out. Most of the people you see on film claim they weren't playing along, but they also didn't have any problem signing the release to use their faces.

WALTON PRICE, *Chief of Police, Hunter's Ridge PD*:

A lot of what they did in those videos was against the law. Chasing the little girl with the knife would have put Lucas behind bars. That's why no one's ever seen him again. Don't believe this ghost story crap. The kid was a punk and he ran off to stay out of trouble.

GARY PINCIOTTI, *Producer*:

We had to cut out a lot of the cursing. Even if they were going for a hard 'R,' it was too much. They were just swearing constantly. It was lazy writing.

DUNTON:
That's just how we talked. This is real. You have to believe me.

PINCIOTTI:
The cursing was fine on the Internet where it's the Wild West, but we wanted to get it down to a PG-13 so we could open on an extra thousand screens for the theatrical release. So we tried to bring the boys into the studio to do ADR, get some better dialogue in there while we were at it. But they wouldn't play.

BELANGER:
I took their money, but I wasn't going to participate in making it fake. Then nobody would believe us.

Look, people have been trying to "catch" me admitting that we staged the whole thing for ten years. That's the most popular question: If we were just trying to get a couple of seconds of footage, why did we record four hours' worth of us screwing around? And why did we keep recording, even when everything went haywire? It's exhausting.

DUNTON:
The answer is, we didn't know how to use the HeadCams. We just synced them to the cloud and left them running.

BELANGER:
My cell phone bill that month was insane.

At the hour-twenty mark of the final cut, the sun has dropped below the horizon and the sky is a shifting palette of fire orange and navy blue. Lucas is seen approaching the bulkhead entrance to the garage of a home at the edge of the forest. He grabs both bulkhead doors and starts shaking them violently, causing a thunderous metal clang. The homeowner—a heavyset man in camouflage*—emerges from the house with a shotgun and chases Lucas away. The other boys turn and run, too—into the woods. This is where the real horror begins.

*the homeowner is the only featured extra in the film who refused to sign a release allowing Sunrise Studios to use his image. As a

consequence, his face and some defining features of his home are intentionally blurred.

PART IV

"I still can't figure out how they did it."
At this point in the film, our heroes have retreated to the woods at the edge of Hunter's Ridge and are on a collision course with their big moment. What happens over the next twenty minutes of film time would cement "Year of the Clowns" as one of the most famous horror films of the 21st Century, and spawn a decade-long debate over how, exactly, they pulled it off. For their part, Dunton and Belanger aren't talking.

BELANGER:
This part is still hard for me to talk about. But it's all there, on the tape.

Sean and Jason are both visibly disturbed by the events of the night. Sean takes off his wig and begins to use his shirt to wipe the makeup off of his face. Lucas asks what he's doing, and Sean tells him they need to ditch the costumes before the police show up. Jason uses his wig to wipe his face, and ditches his shirt. They look around, trying to get a bearing on their surroundings.

DUNTON:
We ran into the woods for a while. You tend to do that when someone is pointing a gun at you.

BELANGER:
I can't speak for the other guys, but I was terrified. Lucas didn't understand why we wanted to stop. He was getting so mad. We tried to tell him, "Dude, it was fun but we're definitely gonna get caught, just chill out," but he kept getting madder.

DUNTON:
When he took off his mask, I thought he was gonna hit Jay. But he just wanted to smoke up.

BELANGER:
You know what happened next.

Lucas tips his mask backwards and lets it rest on his head while he digs a small pipe out of his coat pocket. He lights it, takes a long draw of marijuana smoke, blows it out and takes another. He holds his breath again, and lets the smoke creep out in a long, slow cloud. And that's when he sees the other clown.

BELANGER:
Lucas saw him first. He pointed out to the woods.

Another person in a clown costume has appeared in the moonlight, crossing through a clearing fifty yards deeper in the woods. Skirting between the trees. Watching them.

DUNTON:
We figured it was one of those kids from the car earlier —or maybe a member of a completely separate clown cabal. Regardless, Lucas— who, mind you, had spent the whole night menacing the community—had just taken off his mask in front of a witness.

BELANGER:
That couldn't stand.

Lucas pulls his knife from the holster. "Hey!" Lucas shouts toward the clown. The clown doesn't budge, and as the boys close in a little we get a better look at it. The clown is short, maybe five foot six, and wearing a more traditional costume: baggy, polka dotted jumpsuit, white face paint with a big red smile and blue circles around the eyes, red hair jutting out in cones from the sides and in a puffy ball on top. Lucas starts walking toward him, knife in his grip, taking long, purposeful strides. "Hey buddy, come here!" he calls. After a few seconds, the clown turns and runs. He vanishes from the moonlight of the opening into the forest, and Lucas breaks into a run behind him. Jason and Sean follow, urging Lucas to let the person go.

The camera is shaky during this portion, but you can see just enough:

Lucas barreling into the forest, catching fleeting glimpses of the little clown ahead, dodging between trees and down over hills and across leaf-covered puddles as he leads them deeper into the woods. At one point, he vanishes. They all stop running. Sean and Jason are calling after Lucas to forget about it, but he is furious and unwilling to listen to reason. Jason spots the clown—somehow, on the other side of the clearing—and they give chase again.

DUNTON:
It looked like it was a little kid. We weren't worried about the clown. We were worried about Lucas killing the clown. At first, anyway.

BELANGER:
I was a little worried about the clown.

They have been running for at least five minutes now, directly into the woods. But the clown is slowing down; he has dropped his pace from a run to a casual jog, and then a walk. Lucas pulls the mask back down over his face as he approaches his prey, anxiously wiping the blade of the knife back and forth against his pant leg. Sean and Jason stay back a few paces, pleading now for Lucas to leave the guy alone.

"Turn around," Lucas says. The clown turns his whole body slowly, until the two are looking directly at each other. His face is expressionless, his eyes dark and beady.'

"You're not supposed to be out here," Lucas says. His voice is shaking a little. The audio from this scene, played over black, closed out the iconic trailer for Year of the Clowns.

The little clown looks old under the pancake makeup, much older than the high school punks in the car from earlier; and as his lips curl up into a knowing smirk, we see that his teeth are stained black and jagged sharp. Lucas takes a step back as the clown approaches, and holds the knife out toward him. "Don't make me, man," he stammers.

The clown's hand shoots out and grabs Lucas's wrist. We immediately hear bones crunch; the studio and filmmakers both insist that this is not a sound effect. Lucas howls in pain, drops the knife to the ground. Lucas's sleeve clings to his skin like its being sucked by a vacuum. The cameras shake violently as the boys are startled by what's happening. When they focus on Lucas again, the little clown is gone.

The tightening spreads all the way up his arm and across his chest, then down the other sleeve and his torso, and down his pants until the costume is clinging so tightly that it's indistinguishable from his body. Neither camera moves; Sean and Jason will later say they were both paralyzed with fear, but it's also remarkably controlled footage.

Lucas lets out a gurgle as the sensation moves up beyond his collar and onto the mask, which is sucking directly against the skin of his neck. The mask warps as it pulls in tighter around his features. The eyeballs spring wide open in a demented, offset bulge, and then—amazingly—they blink. Black, with white pupils. There is life in them now. The nose closes around his, collapsing into a bumpy hook. Lucas brings his hands up to his face to try to claw the mask off. What he hasn't realized—but we can see—is that he now has full control of the elongated fingers on his vampire gloves, as if they're his own; the fingernails are as sharp as cut glass. He grabs at the mask and runs the nails down the cheeks. Green-black blood seeps out of the wounds. It is not a mask anymore. It is his own skin.

Lucas drops to his knees, throws his long, clawed fingers behind his head and pulls at the tufts of gray hair behind his crooked new ears— hard enough until it comes out in his fists—and he screams.
But it doesn't sound like screams of pain, or fear.

It sounds like laughter.

BELANGER:
That's when I finally started running. I've never watched the end of the movie for a bunch of reasons, but the biggest one is I can never hear that laugh again. It was inhuman. It was unholy.

PETE SILVER, *Editor:*
I've watched those fourteen seconds of footage more than 300 times. I still can't figure out how they did it.

DUNTON:
We didn't "do" anything. It was real.

SILVER:
There's no CGI. We'd be able to tell. It's a mix of practical effects and editing. Basically they had to make a bunch of variations of that costume, and keep cutting the camera so Lucas can change into the different costumes as he transformed. Otherwise it would be impossible for the eyes to move, for the hands to work, for the blood to look so real. But for the life of me, I can't find the cuts. Filming something like that outside, it would take hours, with no control over the elements. But the lighting is perfect the whole time. There's never a hint of a tonal change. I started zooming in on individual leaves on the trees, looking for one of them to suddenly change position. It never happens.

JEFFREY GORMAN, *Academy Award Winning Makeup and Visual Effects Director*:
Pete Silver and I have been arguing about this for years. He says it's not CGI. I say it has to be, because it can't be prosthetics. Cuts or no cuts, we still probably can't make it look that clean today. I mean, those eyes . . .

GARY PINCIOTTI, *Producer*:
They're geniuses.

GORMAN:
I offered them each a hundred grand to tell me how they did it. Neither one of them returned the call. I went up to 250K. Jason Belanger called back and said, "You're asking the wrong guy. Go out in the woods and ask the clown how he did it." They're kind of jerks, honestly.

The boys run. Sean looks back, long enough for us to see Lucas standing again—watching them silently. He has the knife in his hand. Sean curses, hits Jason in the arm, tells him to look. Jason turns around. The clearing is empty. He looks forward again, and off in the distance we catch a fleeting glimpse of Lucas in a whole different part of the woods, walking between trees. This desperate escape continues for seven minutes, with glimpses of Lucas hunting them at the edge of the frame. They find the street. Screeching laughter echoes in stereo.

PART V

"I guess I wouldn't believe us, either."

The boys return to a civilization that doesn't believe their story. But it finds a home online.

DUNTON:
We went straight to the police. We tried to tell them someone attacked Lucas in the woods and he turned into a clown. We weren't making any sense, but Chief Price sent an officer out to check on it anyway. Finally I got logged into the video stream and played back the footage from the woods.

WALTON PRICE, *Police Chief*:
Friggin' kids.

BELANGER:
He thought it was a prank.

PRICE:
I'd expect it from Jarrett. That kid was no good since junior high. But not the other two. They were good boys. Sean Dunton volunteered every summer at the Meals on Wheels with his mom. I told them to get the hell out and stop wasting our time.

DUNTON:
I guess I wouldn't believe us, either.

BELANGER:
The police weren't taking us seriously, so we dumped the whole thing online. A kid from Sean's school loved it. He did the first rough cut. Other people who found the footage made their own versions. It ran around the Internet for two years before Sunrise bought the rights.

DUNTON:

No one ever came around asking where Lucas went. We declared him a missing person so they would investigate.

PRICE:

He was a dealer, and not just pot. He was hooked in with some bad dudes. He either ran off, or he got himself killed. But he didn't get turned into a ghost clown. I can guarantee you that.

PART VI

The end—or is it?

Sunrise Studios bought the rights to the footage from Dunton and Belanger for $25,000 apiece in 2018. The studio released Year of the Clowns *in theaters in 2019, earning over $300 million worldwide and spawning countless sequels, homages and ripoffs.*

Sean Dunton moved to Portland, Maine after college. He works for a website design company. Jason Belanger lives in Boston, Massachusetts and sells medical diagnostic products. Neither has ever worked in film again. To this day, both remain steadfastly dedicated to their version of the story: that the events in Year of the Clowns *are real.*

GARY PINCIOTTI, *Producer:*

Good for them. I mean, that's why it works, right? It's almost two hours long, and there's really just one big scare. The rest of it is just mood and foreshadowing. I think the minute those boys admit that it's fake—or Lucas Jarrett comes out of hiding—everyone will realize it's not really that scary. It's just clowns.

Editor's Note: Since the events of Year of the Clowns *in 2016, vanishings in the woods around Hunter's Ridge have more than tripled. At least two people have disappeared in the forest every year for the past twelve years.*

Travis Kennedy lives in Scarborough, Maine. His work was recognized in the Best American Mystery Stories *anthology by Houghton Mifflin Harcourt; and has been featured in* Ellery Queen Mystery Magazine, Suspense Magazine *(scheduled),* McSweeney's Internet Tendency, *and* Level Best Books' Best New England Crime Stories *anthology.*

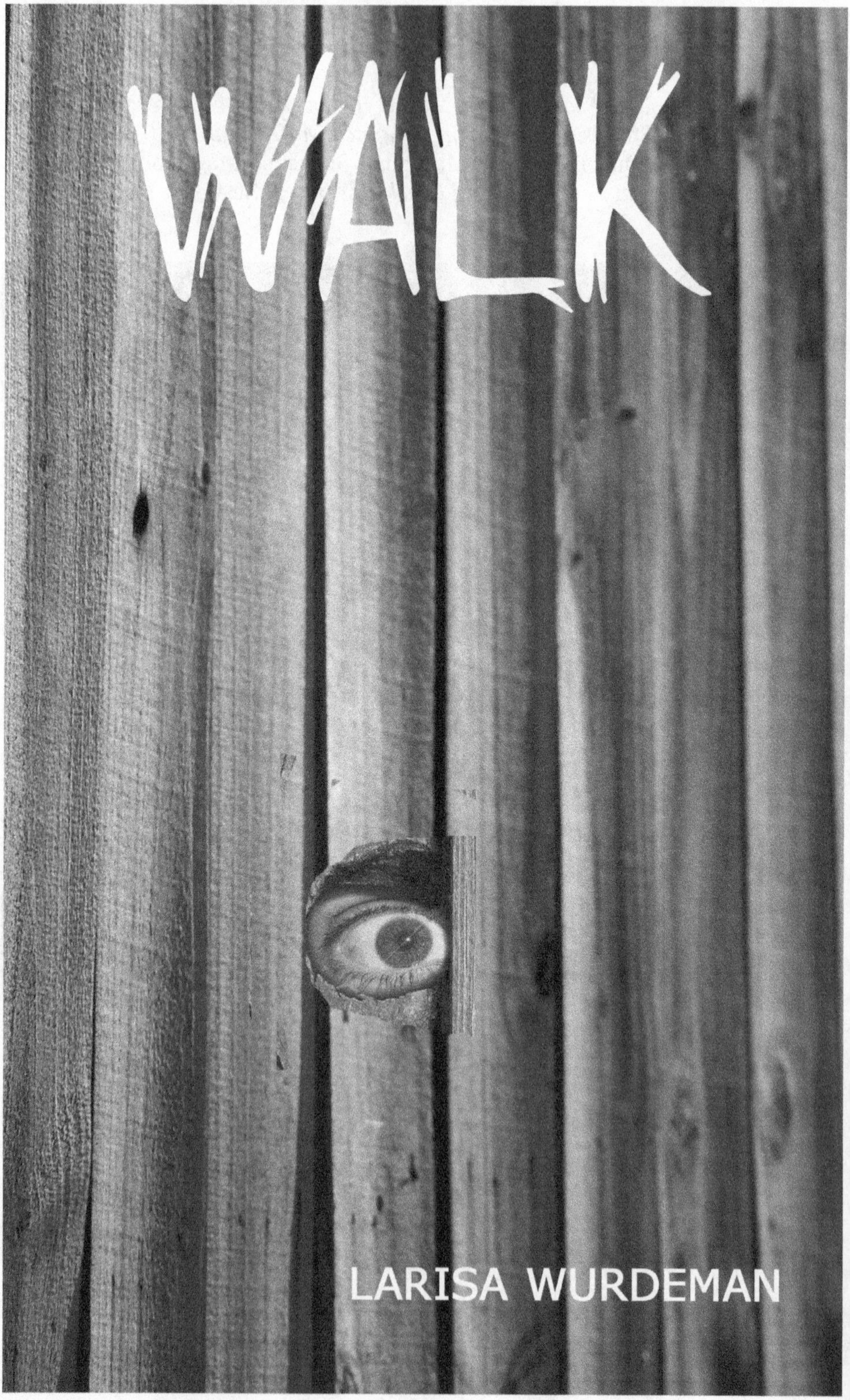
WALK
LARISA WURDEMAN

T HERE'S THIS HOUSE I pass on my way to the bus stop which has a dog that barks all day long.

I only hear it for maybe sixty seconds every day, but I am positive it doesn't ever stop. There are a few reasons why I'm sure of this.

One: the breed. I don't actually know what breed it is. I'm not a fucking dog expert. It's bigger than a chihuahua, smaller than a lab. Isn't as wrinkled as a pug, or as stubby as a wiener-dog. Fur longer than a rat terrier's, but overall uglier than a Pomeranian. And the owners don't seem like the type to buy purebred celebrity ratdogs. I can tell by their 8-foot chain-link fence, and the big mismatched plywood scrap boards leaned against it to ward off nosy pedestrians.

Normally I'm not the type of guy to shamelessly peek through a stranger's fence slats. I might, however, glance over every single day, twice a day, as long as there's no one else around. So it took a while to glean anything from between the gaps.

A couple weeks after I'd first noticed the barking (it was hard to miss), I concluded: the dog was some world's muttiest mutt, and it never shut up. The next logical question: why that was so.

Evidence two: the yard. Specifically, the lack of food, water, or external stimulation. This one might have been more obvious, except I had spent so many days looking for signs of life, and only had a few square feet of yard in view before I'd gone too far as to stare inconspicuously. There was a pole, encased in concrete in an old tire, with a cord connecting it to a tetherball. When it rained, water would pool in the base; maybe the dog drank from this, though I'd never witnessed it (drinking water would mean it would stop barking). There were a couple pots filled with dirt. Others filled with dandelions. An upended tricycle, speared through with more weeds and tall grass. Lots of grass. Piles of dirt and two-by-fours. Something that could have been a greyish rubber chew toy, but might easily have been a rock.

In all, nothing to stimulate even the most boring, tired, terminally-ill dog. Clearly not enough for this yippy-ass ten-pounds-soaking-wet mutt.

Around late October, I learned the house was clearly not abandoned. It was getting dark earlier in the evenings, so I noticed, sometimes, light from the sliding glass door creating long shadows on the unmowed lawn Sometimes these shadows would move. They'd be mirrored by an equally shapeless form in the glass, moving from one side to the other and back A few times I made out something like an arm.

It was hard to hear anything above the puppy's shrill bark. Maybe a low grumble of TV. A couple times I thought I could make out a human voice, but it could also have been my brain playing tricks, desperate for an answer.

Beyond that, I never made out any details about the house's owners. What they looked like, what clothes they wore. All my knowledge (which was literally useless, why was I doing this) was gained obliquely, one inference at a time. They paid the bills. They didn't go outside. They left earlier than me in the morning, or else slept in later, but were always home before rush hour.

Eventually it got so cold I didn't want to prolong my walk for even a few heartbeats. Head tilted down against the wind, I stuffed my hands in my parka and kept a steady pace, desperate to get my blood moving and generate some body heat. The barking was so muffled through the hat pulled over my ears, it was easily ignored.

Nothing else changed.

But something tugged on my conscience, after the first snow flurry and whenever the morning frost glinted in my periphery. I felt inexplicably bad rushing home as fast as possible, though I had no other immediate responsibilities and it was cold as hell.

On impulse, I bought some treats from the corner store. This wasn't the first time I considered tossing the yippy-dog something, but its continued existence proved someone must feed it. I couldn't justify it as a true gift, as the dog was annoying as hell, and honestly, thinking about it too much made me anxious.

Approaching the plywood slats that evening, I paused—the usual yellow rectangle of light stretched across the yard. For reasons I couldn't articulate, I would rather the owners not see me.

But it was pitch-dark out, and the edge of the fence seemed well-enough obscured. I bent down.

The dog was there, of course, and its bark seemed neither hostile nor friendly, nor especially curious. It was doing its duty. It stuck its feet through the slats, then on the ground and back up, nudged a nose in and out. I pulled a biscuit from my pocket.

It paused for just an instant, looked down and back up. In that space of time it gave a sense of true intelligence.

I was so startled that before I could move, a wet mouth snatched the treat from my fingers, swallowed it whole and resumed barking and jumping, over and over, like nothing happened.

My heart was pounding, for some reason. The animal was inches away.

For the first time, I had a chance to study it—its face was flatter than I'd thought, eyes closer together, lighter brown. Its fur was either sparse or so dense it didn't even look like fur. Something was wrong.

Then it paused again. I couldn't look away.

Its individual features looked dog-like, could be said to resemble those of a dog, maybe, but its face—only the face—was unquestionably human.

It blinked twice before I jerked to my feet and ran, shivering, focusing on putting one foot in front of the other.

From then on, I took a different route home.

Larisa Wurdeman lives in Seattle and writes once in a while. She has a degree in linguistics and spends most of her time teaching grammar to computers.

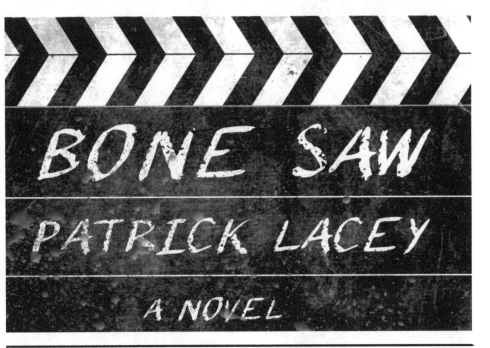

BONE SAW

PATRICK LACEY

A NOVEL

Love
Finds a
Way

LAURA DEHAAN

"**S**OMETHING'S GOT THE cat pregnant."

"Good for the cat," said Biles Munifence, the carnival owner. He leafed through a tattered romance novel, scanning for the words 'breasts,' 'engorged' and 'sodden'. "Who's the proud papa?"

Havelock the carnival barker, only mildly deformed, twisted his hat in his hands. "Dunno, boss. Haven't seen no other cats around."

"That's cats," said Biles. He waved a foot at the barker by way of dismissal, one hand occupied with his belt buckle. "Maybe we'll get another two-headed marvel, eh? Like mother, like child. Damn things will want their own poster next." Havelock hesitated at the door. "Well, go on!" Biles snapped, his hand in his pants.

"Just don't know how a cat could get in with her, with her not able to get out," Havelock mumbled.

"Love finds a way!" Biles roared. "Or it would if you'd afford me the same privacy you give that cat! Out! Vanish! Vamoose!"

Havelock spun around and let the trailer door shut behind him. He rammed his porkpie hat onto his head, covering the stunted black horn that grew from his brow.

"What'd he say?" whispered Loquacia, the mistress of the menagerie, alpha to her animals and less than delta to her own kind.

He shrugged. "Light a cigar."

She nibbled at her thumbs. "How do you think it happened?"

"The usual way. Or maybe it was a *cat burglar*—they're good at getting in and out!" He laughed sharply at his own wit. "I said I'd give him the news and I did. Beat it, kid, and keep a better eye on your babies next time." He turned on his heel and, whistling the first bars of 'Plant a Radish,' left her, a tiny thing in a leopard-print bra with her fingers plucking uselessly at the air.

***

"Boss, the cat's given birth."

"Have a cigar." Biles gestured in the vicinity of his medicine cabinet. "Wish I'd seen it, but the sight of blood makes me woozy. Moggett squeeze out any keepers?"

"Yeah. One. You'd better come see it."

"Only one? Lazy cat." Biles stacked a pile of receipts on his desk and slammed variously geographical snow globes on top to hold them down. "Smile, Havelock, can't you? A birth is a joyous occasion."

Havelock contorted his mouth obediently. "We got an extra tank around? Like for the mermaid display?"

"Somewhere, sure, check the crates. Why, did hers break?"

"No," said Havelock. There was a crowd of carnies around the menagerie tent who stepped aside as Biles approached.

"Damn good money I paid that taxidermist," Biles waved genially to his employees. "Body of a macaque, tail of a salmon, breasts of . . . you know, I never did ask where he got the breasts. Cow udders, perhaps. Ah, and here's the proud family!" . Loquacia sat in a pile of straw with two-headed Moggett nestled beside her. The cat's heads took turns licking the little bundle of fluff that peeped and cheeped uncertainly.

Biles leaned down to give the fluff an appraising look. "One head. Waste of a talent.Hey, you, you," he snapped his fingers at Loquacia. "Why've you got that thing in a bowl instead of curled up next to its mother? It'll catch a chill."

"It needs to be in water," said Loquacia. "Its bottom bit, at least."

"Some animal guru you are."Biles lifted the kitten out of the bowl. Moggett hissed and swiped at him. To his credit, he didn't drop her baby, even when its fish tail flicked water right in his eye.

***

"This isn't possible," said Biles. He, Havelock and Loquacia were in her trailer, Moggett and her baby comfortably situated on an overstuffed pillow on the floor with a towel under the kitten's bowl for easy mopping-up. Biles and Havelock and Loquacia were less comfortably situated on a loveseat built for two. "It isn't possible and it isn't funny. Where'd you get the fish, Loquacia?"

"She didn't sew it together," said Havelock. Loquacia shook her head with tiny, emphatic shakes. "This isn't some taxidermy trick like the mermaid. It's real and it's alive."

Biles, when he shook his head, shook his entire upper body. Now it rotated like the agitator in a washing machine. "No. No. Loquacia, I can't believe you'd hurt one of your animals by sewing half a fish onto it. Who did it for you?"

"It's not a fake, boss," said Havelock.

Biles put his hand over Havelock's mouth. "That same person must have fed Moggett up for a while, got her nice and fat, convinced you she was pregnant, then when the time was right slipped the fishy-kitten beside her and *pow*! Miracle baby! Oh, it's gotta be a fake. You can't breed 'em like that!"

"Moggettalawny," whispered Loquacia.

"What? What? Speak up!"

"I named it Moggettalawny. I dunno if it's a boy or a girl, but I thought the name would work for both."

Havelock pushed Biles's hand out of his face. "It'll sell tickets, boss."

"Animal cruelty, that's what people will think we're selling. Who the hell is the father?"

"Well, the mermaid's a stiff and we got no other fish around," said Havelock. "So that narrows it down."

"To somewhere left of impossible," grumbled Biles. "Well, if it lives, it lives, and much happiness to it. We should at least wait until it's weaned before we start shouting its existence. Make sure it's alive and thriving before we have every damn scientist and her mother coming around. See how it does in show business before selling it to the highest bidder—"

In a flash Biles's head was forcibly wrenched to the level of Havelock's crotch by means of Loquacia's fist balled up in his fancy cravat. "If you sell my baby, I'll kill you," she said.

"I respect your position and the feeling behind it," Biles said, somewhat muffled. "You have raised an excellent point and I would not dream of separating you from your beloved companions. Please may I have my neck back."

Loquacia let him go and Biles straightened up with a splendid amount of cracks and grunts. Havelock made minute adjustments to his pants and brushed off his lap. "I'll tell the others to keep their mouths shut about this until we get your say-so, boss," he said. "Until then, it might be best if we keep the kitten in here with Moggett and Loquacia."

"Agreed," said Biles. Loquacia nodded, a tiny thing once more.

***

"Boss."

Biles's head lay on his desk. Empty bottles glinted around him. "No."

"Boss, it's the chicken."

"No."

"She musta hid one of her eggs."

"No."

"'Cause it hatched."

"I don't want to hear it."

"Into a snake."

"Havelock, I don't want to hear it."

"With a beak."

"GOD." One hand rose to point a finger at the barker. "DAMMIT." The hand sank back down.

Havelock eased his way into Biles's trailer and stepped around the stacks of romance novels and empty jars smelling faintly of pickles. "Loquacia says it's doing well."

"It's a plucked chicken," Biles said. "Just a dang plucked chicken we made wear a sweater. It's dumb. It's funny. It's *ordinary*. The snake is literally half a snake Loquacia saved from a bicycle accident and it uses a plastic tube to collect its waste. It doesn't even have its damn genitals anymore! How in the hell reserved for my father does a snake with no genitals mate with a hen?"

"They both have a cloaca," said Havelock.

"That is wonderful news. They share a cloaca. And before you try showing off, Havelock, I am aware that *cloaca* is Latin for *sewer*, and one of them is *missing it*."

"The lion and lamb hybrid made a certain Biblical sense," said Havelock.

"I am certain that when the Good Book mentions the lion laying down with the lamb, it was *not* meant, as you say, Biblically."

"I don't get it," Havelock admitted. "Loquacia doesn't get it either, and she's the closest to any of the critters."

"She holds a certain fondness for you, I've noticed," Biles said, his face finally creeping out from its hiding place amongst newspaper crossword puzzles. "I am positive she knows more than she says, even if she says almost nothing as a daily activity. If you could butter her up, sweeten her disposition . . . "

"That's a lousy thing to do to a lady, I don't care *what* condiments you want me to use," said Havelock.

"I am not suggesting you become another stud in her menagerie! Merely being available should she wish to . . . extol the pleasures of motherhood." Biles, rolled his wrists in suggestive circles. "Unless you're truly eager to see how many secret mutations a circus can hold. We can't keep them hidden forever, and Loquacia, bless her well-intentioned heart, is no match for a squadron of journalists."

Havelock sighed. "Nor are most of us. All right, I'll see what I can get out of her. Boss. You don't really think she has anything to do with it, do you? Little Loquacia?"

Biles picked up a sheet of newsprint and wiped sadly at the drool stains. "We already have one animal fancier." "Heaven help us if we've gained two."

***

Havelock had offered Loquacia an invitation to his trailer that evening, but when the door crashed open he was startled to see Tarantella, the Spider Woman, instead.

She covered the room in two broad steps, stamped down, and vogued. Havelock winced when he saw the holes her spiked heels left in the flooring. "You tell your little *Turteltaube*," she snapped, "that if she tries to lick me again, I slap her with *all* my hands." Her parasitic limbs shook with rage.

"Oh god," said Havelock. "She's not my Turteltaube, but what's she done now?"

Tarantella slapped him as a point of emphasis. "I just tell you! She follow me with her tongue, like this, *bleh-leh-leh-leh*, and I slap her, not hard enough. She tell me she love my little legs, which, *ptuuuie*! If you like her running after you, that is between you and white Jesus. But *me*, leave *out*." She absent-mindedly slapped him again, clicked a castanet, and flounced out of his trailer.

She'd been running after him? Oh god, that explained why the clowns kept giggling whenever he walked by. He'd put it down to the simple-minded envy of his elevated position as Biles's right-hand man, but apparently Loquacia's *fondness* was evident to everyone except himself, which did not bode well for the evening.

The screen door opened again, this time with a creak. "Hello?" Loquacia said, staring directly at him. "Havelock?"

"It sure is me," he said, trying to summon up his barker charisma. "Come on in, toots. I've just plumped the cushions."

Loquacia eased into his trailer like it was a cold mountain lake. "I just saw Tarantella come out of here." There was a jealous edge to her voice he hadn't expected.

"Business matters," he said. *Don't lick your coworkers* wasn't a conversation he expected to have, either. "Don't worry about it. I wanted to talk about *you*."

Her tight little face softened and he mentally kicked himself in the rear for being such a heel. "Oh golly, me? What about me?" She skirted the edge of the room and perched on a milk crate.

"Well, your kids," he said hastily. "Who are great! They're all really, really . . . great. So great, I can hardly believe how they happened. Without you." Subtlety in discourse was not a skill he'd ever tried to hone, not when more money was to be made shouting, "YOU WANNA SEE A FISH WITH TITS? HAVE WE GOT A FISH WITH TITS!"

"Oh. Well. They did! I'm just a lucky, lucky girl." She edged closer to him, an impressive feat since she was already half-falling off the milk crate.

"Lucky," he nodded. "Every baby is a lucky baby, isn't it? I mean, what are the chances that two people are going to meet and mate and" *stop talking oh god this is not the direction I wanted to take* "end up with a mockery of God's plan?" he finished lamely.

"Havelock." She went to him swiftly, so swiftly that in his surprise he didn't pull back when she caressed his stubby horn. "You are *not* a mockery of God's plan."

"I didn't say I was," he protested, but she stroked his horn so lovingly that he felt himself shrivel up and die a little.

"You're a beautiful unicorn," she cooed.

A loud, prolongated "OOH!" came from many voices outside and Havelock's attention snapped to the windows which were crowded by the faces of various carnival members.

"Good talk, Loquacia!" he stood so abruptly that she squeaked and fell down. He picked her up with one hand and escorted her directly to the door. "Shine on, you wacky star!" He pitched her outside, yanked the screen door shut, closed the inner door, drew the curtains and snapped off the lamp. He pressed his face into the glass, seeing if he could recognize any of the carnies gleefully scattering, but it was only Loquacia he saw, illuminated by the electric light still buzzing above the door.

Loquacia, her hand halfway in her mouth, licking between her fingers as she stared at the darkness of the trailer.

Havelock looked away, feeling like he'd been caught watching something dirty. When he looked again, she was gone. He hesitated, unnerved, then breathed a swear word and eased himself out of his trailer. It was time to do a little counter-spying.

The other carnies seemed to think the show was over, so he was able to follow her without being spotted. It was no surprise she ended up going back to the menagerie tent. Fortunately Havelock had been with the circus long enough that all of her pets were used to him and, knowing he was a source of neither food nor fondness, ignored him.

She stopped in front of the fake zebras, the off-white horses onto whom Biles had thought to paint black stripes. Loquacia trimmed their manes and repainted the stripes after every show and rub-down. She also, Havelock observed with not a little surprise, was eating their hair.

What in the hell of my own making is she doing?

One handful of trimmed hair went down her gullet, then another. Loquacia scratched the not-zebras behind their ears, carefully inspected the hygiene of their teeth, checked their hooves for any signs of damage. Havelock hunkered down behind a bale of hay and pondered.

The Loquacia coughed up a hairball and he stopped his pondering to focus on not vomiting.

Then he concentrated on not expelling the vomit that snuck up anyway.

Loquacia had taken the handful of sloppy, soggy hair and

imparted it?

impacted it?

impregnated one of the horses with it.

The fake zebra stood calm and unconcerned as Loquacia withdrew her arm, her elbow, her forearm and wrist and emptied hand from its horsey vagina. Its tail swished at a fly. Loquacia gave it a peck on its withers and went away, hopefully to wash up.

As he gagged down the vomitus, he noted his brain's insistence on referring to the clearly female horse as an *it*, probably as a defense mechanism. Was this what Loquacia had been doing the entire time? Eating the discarded detritus of her charges, mixing it with her own bile and juices, hacking it up and shoving it into their unsuspecting wombs?

She'd licked her fingers after touching him.

Havelock shivered and crept away from the menagerie, wondering how long it took a horse to gestate.

***

He didn't tell Biles. There was a difference between showcasing the natural anomalies of the world versus actively creating them and he wouldn't put it past the man to have Loquacia continue her extracurriculars, consequences be damned. Oh, Biles might profess to despise the beaked snake and the fishy kitty, but the carnival owner did love his money and once the weirdness wore off, he'd be putting them on display with the rest of the freaks.

Havelock had to admit, in the cockles of his heart, he had some degree of morbid paternal interest. Would the creature have his eyes? His nose? His bipedal preference?

There was only one way to find out, and the answer lay in the fake zebra's belly. And ultimately, unfortunately, with Loquacia.

He steeled his nerves, dabbed on his best cologne, grabbed a handful of wildflowers and knocked on Loquacia's trailer door.

The lion-lamb hybrid was handling hooves well and despite his leonine face seemed to prefer a diet of grass and straw. The snake was in every way an ordinary snake, albeit one with a beak. A special tank had been crafted for Moggettalawny, who had a kitten's curiosity but also needed to be kept damp, for the sake of its fishy tail, and there was talk of making it a sort of fishbowl wheelchair someday.

"Okay, but," he said, "this zebra thing."

Loquacia giggled. "They're horses, silly."

"They're girls," he continued. "All of them horses are girls. I know turkeys can just drop an egg if they feel like it, but a horse ain't a turkey and a cat and a fish can't do the nasty, especially if one of them's dead. So explain to me this horse thing."

She giggled again, self-consciously this time. "How do you explain a miracle?"

"There was nothing immaculate about these conceptions."

Her goofy grin disappeared. "Love finds a way."

"It's not love, kiddo! You can't just lick my horn and make a baby and call it love!"

She looked at him blankly. "I don't love you, Havelock."

He didn't love her either, but still, *rude*.

"I love my babies," she went on. "I been trying for *years* to have my own babies and now I've found a way to do it."

"You're making monsters!"

"I'm making *babies*."

He gestured wildly, knocking over the flowers he'd brought and Loquacia had stuck into a tissue box. "What happens when one of your kids is born with, with, with a backwards head or feet for ears or they got no lungs or something? What if it can't even *live*?"

"Oh, nonsense, they've all been healthy. They can't help being different."

"Okay, *that's* nonsense! You're actively *making* them different!"

"All right!" she snapped. "So I want my kids to be special! I want to know I was involved! I'm not in some lab torturing a bunny or sewing two heads onto a dog! This is *nature*, it's a *natural* thing, same as a pig farm with artificial insemination! I can throw around those big words, too, you know!"

She huffed and puffed. He took her hands gently, shook them gently, spoke gently. "You gotta promise," he said, "you *gotta* promise, if it goes wrong, you'll stop. Okay? You already got some real beautiful babies, but they need you, okay? You got *so much* love to give, and these kids are gonna need all the love they can get."

Loquacia nodded and wiped away a tear. "All right, Havelock, if anything goes wrong this time, I'll stop making them. But it *won't* go wrong, because I'm a *great* mother."

He patted her hand and couldn't think of a blessed thing to say.

***

"If you've come in to tell me another bundle of misshapen farmflesh is being delivered unto us, I am not interested in hearing it," said Biles as soon as Havelock entered his trailer.

"There is," said Havelock, "but I can see you're busy with your needlepoint, so I'll leave you to it."

Biles stabbed at the fabric ring and scowled. "Supposed to be relaxing," he cursed as the needle pricked his finger. "Supposed to be a beginner piece, too. Beginner, hah! I shudder to think what I'll become when I turn masterclass." He turned it towards Havelock. "What do you think?"

In sloppy red stitches read the words, BLES THIS MESS.

"Looks great, boss," said Havelock. "The misspelling really makes it pop. I'm gonna go check on the zebras."

"They're just horses." Biles threaded another needle. "And it is *not* misspelled!" he shouted as Havelock left. "There's no such thing as wrong spelling! Just wrong thinking!"

"Is he coming?" said Tarantella, who waited with a small crowd of carnies outside the menagerie tent.

"No stomach for it," Havelock muttered. "Just leaves all the messy bits to me."

"Hey, a father should be there for his kid's birth," whispered the sword-swallower and the trapeze artists tittered behind their hands.

Havelock whirled on them. "You lot are the real monsters!"

Each and every face gave him an identical look of unimpressed scorn

"Even sounds like a teen dad," the sword-swallower said and the trapeze artists tittered again.

"Havelock!" came Loquacia's frightened voice from inside the tent. "You gotta help me!"

Anger and embarrassment flushed his face and he hurried inside, cackles and cat-calls following him.

Loquacia was at the horse's rear end, pulling at the spindly hind legs of something decidedly equine. "What's wrong?" he said.

"It ain't moving! Grab that leg an' help me pull. Oh, gosh . . . "

Quickly he took up a place beside her. Hand over hand, they drew the foal out.

"It was s'posed to be a beautiful unicorn," Loquacia whimpered. "I didn't mean for it to be like this."

He had been ready to defend his progeny, half expecting a centaur or some variant of minotaur. What he had not expected, what Loquacia's weeping could not have anticipated, was a wee little pony with the belly and neck of a human child, but a single blunted horn in place of a head.

***

Tap, tap.

"Come in, my child," said Biles.

Havelock entered the trailer with his head hung low. "You wanted to see me?".

Biles wore a back-mounted leaf blower and was pulling on the starter. "Indeed. Can't help but notice we don't have a new baby not-a-zebra."

"No, boss."

"Cook says Loquacia hasn't been to the canteen in a week," said Biles. "Care to tell me why?"

Havelock opened his mouth and Biles revved on the leaf blower, scattering vegetable scraps and loose underwear about. "Say that again," said Biles.

Havelock opened his mouth and Biles blew a stack of romance novels at him. "Absolutely fascinating.I trust you to look after my employees, Havelock. Tarantella is furious, which, granted, is like saying 'water is wet' or 'death comes to us all'. Apparently Loquacia keeps, let me check my notes, *licking* her, and while I could assume that she is now keeping a low profile after the drubbing Tarantella gave her, in my heart of hearts I do not believe in simplicity any more." Biles pointed the leaf blower into a corner and blasted whatever debris dared to remain settled. "You are a *barker*, Havelock. Go bark. Woof, woof."

Havelock slunk out with his tail between his legs.

***

Havelock knew the logical choices to see Loquacia would be at the menagerie or her trailer, but as Biles stated, simplicity was not the reliable friend it once was. Besides, the more intel he gathered from the rest of the carnies, the longer he could put off another interview with the chit.

Nearly everyone merely giggled or shrugged when he asked after her, but one clown offered that they had seen her down by the Pit. "Not just to have a pee, mind. She was poking around the spider webs, catching 'em and putting 'em into jars."

"The webs?"

"Naw, the spiders."

First the Spider Lady and now actual spiders? "She promised she'd *stop*," Havelock moaned. The clown rolled their eyes and waved dismissively as Havelock dashed to the Pit. It was where the human and animal waste of the circus ended up and it always boasted a healthy colony of spiders, due to the number of flies the excreta attracted. Though he was no forensic araneologist, it did look like there were fewer spiders than usual, and all the webs were torn apart.

Armed with that information, Havelock trudged to Loquacia's trailer and knocked on the flimsy door. "Loquacia. It's Havelock. Let me in?"

"Go away," she yelled. Then, quieter, "It's open."

Havelock let himself in, treading carefully to avoid the various smatterings of scat and vomit. Though the various hybrids had finally been given permanent housing in the menagerie tent, it didn't look like Loquacia had done much to tidy up after them. "Loquacia," he said, and was about to follow up with something pointed and incisive, yet sympathetic and understanding, but instead he let out a high-pitched shriek.

Loquacia rubbed her distended, purple stomachs. "Hi, Havelock," she said. "Keep it down, you're upsetting my babies."

Havelock sank to the floor, the carpet no longer a concern. "How many babies?" he squeaked. Yards and yards of loose yarn were tumbled about her legs and arms, highlighting her bare torso and the fist-sized protrusions sticking out like burls on a tree.

"Um . . . it's my first time, but . . . " Loquacia patted each lump. "Fifty? A hundred each?"

"A hundred what?"

Loquacia shifted on the loveseat. "Spiders."

"WHY SPIDERS?"

Her flesh visibly rippled. "Shut up a minute, would ya?" One skinny hand pushed damp hair from her cheek, another rubbed a towel across her sweaty chest, *another* scratched her leg . . .

"What'd you do to yourself, kid?" Havelock whispered.

"You're so smart, you tell me," she said. "Nobody thinks I can put more than two an' two together, and by the way *duh* I *know* 'The Spider Lady' is just a stage name, I wasn't *after* her because of *that, geez.* I just thought maybe I'd grow a twin on the inside that'd give me more wombs or stomachs or something. The extra arms are nifty, too. And this *is* the last time, so don't worry about it." She brushed at an angry tear. "I'm *going* to be a *mother*, Havelock, and I am going to be the *best* mother and my babies are going to be *strong* and *beautiful*."

"Your babies are going to be *spiders!*"

"*Strong, beautiful* spiders."

He groped for an argument. "You're gonna *die!*"

She smiled.

"I learned something neat," she said. "It's what made me decide on spiders. Some of the moms, right, they love their babies *so, so* much that they give themselves up as their babies' first meal." Her body spasmed, flesh rippling like river water. "They just tug on the webs and *oops!* The vibrations attract the babies to the mommy, just like she was any other prey in the web, and then it's slurp, slurp, slurp! Vibrations are like spanking, but less mean." Her head lolled and with a visible effort she raised it up to stare at Havelock. "I would never spank my kids."

Another spasm gripped her, each limb and lump straining in a different direction. One by one, the stomach-wombs peeled open and dozens, hundred, *thousands* of tiny precise legs groped towards the trailer's fluorescent light. From the ragged wounds, watery blood mixed with a yellowish fluid which ran in ribbons down the loveseat.

Still the spiderlings poured out, mincing prettily over the ruins of their mother, inspecting with curiosity the yarn crisscrossing Loquacia's limbs. She laughed as their legs prickled her face.

"Hello, my babies!"

The yarn trembled.

Though he couldn't see the details, the results of a thousand minute nips blossomed on Loquacia's body, followed by a thousand threads of running blood. And another thousand as the spiderlings took a second bite, and another thousand with a third...

Havelock stumbled out of the trailer and bellowed for Biles while the other carnies clucked their tongues and shook their heads and pointed him in different directions, but Havelock followed the sound of the leaf blower and grabbed Biles by the shoulders, ignoring his blustered questions and steering him to Loquacia's trailer.

"What in the hell of my mother's creation?" said Biles softly, too shocked to scream.

"She's in there," Havelock sobbed, pointing at the loveseat whose occupant was already covered in a mush of silken spurtings and fluid unknown to man.

"Right," said Biles. He rolled up his sleeves, pulled on the starter and with an unearthly howl unleashed the full fury of a 63.3 cc 2-stroke 234 MPH leaf blower on the spider babies.

***

The dust settled.

Havelock stood with his arms and legs extended like a super model's and tried not to inhale deeply. "Do you have any idea how much shit and piss was embedded in the carpets?"

"Give a man a leaf blower and every problem looks like a leaf," said Biles. "I did what I could with the information you gave me. Now what the hell is going on?"

Havelock sneezed and rubbed his nose. "I can explain," he said and sneezed again. "God, this dust." He started to brush off his chest but froze when a movement on the back of his hand caught his eye.

"Biles," he said.

But Biles was inspecting his own hands, and forearms, and everywhere else he could see. "Havelock," Biles said, in the same tone of voice.

Crawling daintily over them, refreshed by the leaf blower whose mighty power did little more than send their light-as-a-sigh bodies on a lovely airborne adventure, Loquacia's children excitedly explored the fresh meat right under their feet.

"Shittery fuck," said Biles.

"Hello!" piped the spider babies, Loquacia's tiny face beaming from each one. "Hello! Hello, my babies! Hello!"

Laura DeHaan is very quiet and definitely not behind you. For a full listing of her work, visit https://iaminyoureyebrain.com

RUN THE TABLE

CODY GOODFELLOW

HOYT SAT WITH Lars Brewer in the parking lot out front of Ringo's Billiards in Lars's primer-black 1970 El Camino. Rain drummed on the roof and leaked in through a crack in the windshield to drip on the dashboard.

"What do you need me to do?"

"Just back my fucking play." Hoyt banged the fiberglass cast on his right forearm against the dashboard. "You got a piece?"

Lars shook his shaggy head. "Fuck no."

"Can you *act* like you do?"

Lars shrugged. He still carried his brass knuckles, a souvenir from his debt collection days, and a knife in his boot, but if he had to deploy either of these, the situation was already fucked beyond repair. He knew that a cooly projected assurance of violence would keep the other side from fucking things up.

Lars didn't need to ask who the other side was.

Harley Vickers owned a tire and car stereo shop on Lombard, but people said he ran this gang of tweaker crust punks who did B&E's all over the north end and sold him the sport wheels and stereos and shit he resold, and sabotaged anything they couldn't take with them, so his victims ended up becoming customers. Whether or not this scheme earned out, he had plenty of time to perfect his pool game, and was reigning champ in every local tourney.

The whole neighborhood knew about how Hoyt called out Vickers at the monthly nine-ball tournament at Sam's Hollywood Billiards last month, accusing him of cheating and challenging him to a thousand-dollar side series, best of five. They were split 2-2 and both gunning for the 9 when Hoyt bent over to pick up his chalk and some overeager flunky of Harley's stomped his right hand and broke it, arguably causing Vickers to scratch. Lars was working the door that night, and personally had to eject Vickers's posse and drive Hoyt to the ER.

Hoyt had won the city-wide trick shot competition three years running and went to the Pac-West Invitational last year, though he was disqualified for reasons never made clear. Lars figured it must've been drugs, the way Hoyt ran his mouth and scratched under his cast with a nail file. Lars knew those things could get itchy, but Hoyt went at it with a will, as if he didn't care he must be shredding his skin. The doctor said he'd have full function when the cast came off in a month, but the game couldn't wait. Hoyt was living in his car, which was now up on cinderblocks because someone (surprise, surprise) had stolen the wheels off it. Vickers was talking shit all over town, even accusing Hoyt of faking the broken hand to welsh on the bet, and he'd be unable to shark at a dump like this for beer money, if he didn't defend his name.

As they approached the pool hall, Hoyt, with his cue in its carrying case under his good arm, hung back so Lars had to open the door for him. It was quiet inside and darker than a coal miner's asshole, except for the pools of grimy lamplight on apple-green felt. Three tweakers abruptly stopped pushing the balls around in an inept cutthroat game on a front table, and the cashier abruptly realized something was burning in the kitchen.

At least he understood why they'd picked Ringo's. Both these potatoheads were banned from Sam's, and this was the only other pool hall in town where you were guaranteed not to draw an audience. A strip-mall shithole deep on the wrong side of 82nd, Ringo's had fourteen shabby Brunswick coin-op tables that retained the balls so you couldn't pull table-scratches, making it a non-starter for any serious game. Way in the back, in a gallery behind a beaded curtain stood the only tournament-grade table in the place; but nobody ever played on it.

The scuffed felt was faded pale pink and stained with beer and grease, the rails grubby and scarred from when they used to let you smoke inside; but anyone with an eye could tell the table was a grand old custom job, with walnut inserts, genuine ivory diamond-sights and a superbly smooth, meticulously level slate bed. Whoever had commissioned it must've been a dwarf, however, for the table was barely two-and-a-half feet tall. The owner had looked into getting the legs extended, but in the end just put it up on loose bricks.

Every time Lars had ended up here, this table was used as a buffet for foil tubs of slimy buffalo wings from the barbecue place next door, if it was used for anything. Usually, the stained-glass Rainier Beer lamp over the table was dimmed, a chalk-dusted sheet thrown over the felt.

Lars could make out Vickers leaning over the table, idly bouncing the cue ball off the far cushion. Two much bigger men stood behind him, so fucking tall, the lamplight didn't reach their faces.

"I ain't got all night," Vickers bellowed. "Get your welshing ass back here."

Hoyt slipped Lars a ten and ordered him to get a shot of Jameson and a Rolling Rock and play House Of Pain's "Jump Around" on repeat with the change. Lars obliged, but before the jukebox had finished blaring out the opening horn fanfare, a huge Samoan in wraparound shades stormed up and ripped the cord out of the outlet.

Hoyt ambled over and set his case down, opened it and lazily began assembling his cue like an assassin. "Cool your tits, old man," he said, "and show me your money."

Vickers fanned a fistful of hundreds and stuffed it back in his sheepskin jacket. "Show me yours."

Hoyt stalled, patting himself down until Vickers took a sip of his beer and slammed it on a table. When he finally found it, he flashed the roll and started to pocket it again, but Vickers grabbed his hand and tried to force him to drop the cash. Lars, coming back with the drinks, set them down and crowded Vickers. The Samoans crowded *him*.

"I had you dead to rights last time," Vickers said. "You're not leaving with this."

"I'll hold it," Lars said. Hoyt handed over his roll and backed off, chewing a toothpick. Lars riffled it, holding his breath, but it was fifties and hundos all the way through. Tucking it in his breast pocket, he said, "Now give me yours."

"Go to hell," Vickers snarled. "You're his bitch."

"You know me better than that," Lars said, "or you should."

Vickers eyed him for a hot moment, mulling over the situation. "It needs to be someone impartial."

"I'm not his friend. He paid me fifty bucks to watch his back."

"You work cheap."

"I'm not working at all, because nobody's gonna make me. If you both paid me, I'm impartial as fuck."

Looking over the pool hall and realizing neither the tweakers nor the cashier, who'd stepped out for a smoke and some nose-powder, were reliable or impartial, he said, "Fine."

Hoyt elaborately spat out his beer. "You're supposed to be––"

"I am," Lars said, louder than he meant to. "All that's happening here is a few games of pool. Right?"

Vickers handed Lars his stake, and after grappling with his wallet like the cash was coming off his skin, he forked over a couple moist twenties and a ten. "Better not fuck me over . . . "

"Call it in the air." Lars flipped a quarter after proving to both sides that it wasn't a trick coin. Vickers said heads and it came up tails. Hoyt pumped his fist in the air and grabbed his cue.

A true blue-collar pool shark, Hoyt had been wearing the same clothes the last four times Lars saw him, but his pool cue was like a sniper rifle, somehow sleek and subtly contoured though it rolled perfectly on the table when Hoyt tested it. Ebony and creamy ivory inset in a herringbone pattern at the butt, and *Hoyt's Boom Stick* laser-etched in Gothic script down the shaft. Someday, it would be the talk of the local pawn shop.

One of the Samoans—Lars figured his name was Sonny, because it was tattooed across the back of his neck—racked the balls, meticulously sorting and cramming them so tightly into formation that when he lifted the frame, the 1 rolled forward an eighth of an inch. Hoyt protested until Sonny grunted and started over.

Hoyt circled the table, digging in his cast with the file and glaring intently as if one of the pockets owed him money. Even after Sonny had stepped away from the table, Hoyt patiently worked variables in his head, and for once, nobody rushed him.

For anyone who really cared about the game, pool would be a religion, if religion answered prayers. Stripped of all but the rudest physics, the game was a window into a pure world where things did what they were supposed to, mostly, if the men playing were as mechanical as the game. Men who would never know a moment of contentment or fulfillment in their lousy lives could carry on like kings after running a table. People who couldn't balance a checkbook could intuit the hidden geometry necessary to turn the chaotic chatter of balls into a square dance, a conga line into a pocket, and men who couldn't piss in a toilet without hitting their shoes could work magic.

Lars was terrible at the game and never had much patience for the people who played it, but he could well understand why some lived for it, though he was mystified at how they found, for even a little while, some bit of self-control.

But he'd heard things about this table. You never believed, because at the core of every spooky story was an untold kernel of human frailty. Blaming your own shitty skills on a crooked cue or an unstable table was easy, and the excuses took on a life of their own.

A guy who used to work here but now tended bar at Sam's said the real reason they never booked the table was that there were so many arguments, complaints and fights: the kid who smashed his best friend's nose with the 8-ball in a dispute over a table scratch, or the biker who got stabbed and bled out on the floor before the ambulance arrived. To hear them tell it, the table was like the Oregon Vortex; balls never went where they were sent, and tempers flared like a lit match to gasoline. Of course it was all bullshit; if half the stories were true, the felt would be encrusted with blood, and the table clearly hadn't been resurfaced since the Nixon era.

Hoyt finally stopped at the foot of the table, pointed at a near corner pocket and stuck his right hand in it, tapping the cast against the chrome pocket liner and staring at the diamond-formation of balls. Then he set the cue ball on the head spot, leaned over the table and planted his cast on the felt, rested the cue on a notch cut into the fiberglass, between his first and second knuckle.

"This is bullshit," Vickers said.

"You wanted a fair game, your boyfriend shouldn't have gimme this handicap." Lining up, Hoyt pumped the stick once, pulled back and rammed the cue ball with authority. His follow-through was like a designated hitter drilling a fastball into the bleachers, banging his cue off the lamp so the light swayed, seasickish, as the scattering high-compression bakelite balls chased their shadows across the pale pink plain.

When they came to rest, the 9 was not accounted for.

"Cheating little shit," Vickers said.

Sonny moved to rack the balls, but Hoyt pointed his cue at Lars. "You do it."

Lars went over and palmed the 9 out of the corner pocket, but as he did, he watched Hoyt kill his beer and order another. He held his broken arm close to his chest until he got to the table, when he tipped the cast over the empty shot-glass. Blood dripped freely out of the finger-holes. Crazy punk must've slashed himself up good with that nail file. Lars's stomach turned as he reached into the pocket, expecting the liner to be tacky with fresh blood, but the ball came out clean as anything in this dirty town. Gathering up the rest of the balls, he free-handed them into a tight diamond and stepped back for Vickers to break.

Chalking up his slightly more tastefully customized cue—— diamondback pattern with red faux-marble inserts——Vickers pistoned the cue ball with admirable thrust behind it, but the ball wobbled impotently into the 1 and kissed off it to limp away towards the side pocket, dying an inch short of a catastrophic scratch.

Vickers said, "Damned table's crooked."

"Maybe it's your stick," Hoyt said, settling in behind the cue ball. "That's what your wife tells everybody. You wanna forfeit, just say so."

Vickers stared daggers at the kid, but he didn't suggest they change tables or find another venue. He didn't do anything but chew his lower lip as he watched Hoyt pick off the 1 and the 2. Lars could have stopped it, but the room was hot and stank of copper and sweat and, though he could think of no earthly reason why, he had an erection that could scrape ice off a windshield. He couldn't take his eyes off the table, which seemed to be the source of the heat.

Hoyt went over to the side pocket and tapped it with his cast again, smirking. Lars tilted his head, doping it out. He had a clear shot to sink the 3 in the corner, but the side pocket would require some kind of backspin voodoo a man with a busted hand seemed quite incapable of conjuring. He bent over the table and notched his cue on the cast, took a couple pumping pokes just short of the cue ball, teasing it, then jabbed it with surprising force for such a delicate operation.

The cue ball punched the 3 into the cluster and extracted the 9 with a jeweler's precision to send it towards the side pocket. The Samoans inhaled half the air out of the room. Vickers cursed wordlessly and Hoyt had started to do a little dance when the 9 tapped the bumper just to the left of the pocket and came to rest, precariously hanging on the edge.

"*Motherfucker!*" Hoyt screamed and raised his fist. Lars launched off his stool and caught his arm before he could pound the table in a clear attempt to shake the ball loose.

"You think I'm new?" Vickers growled, and Lars looked at him as if he'd forgotten he was here. Vickers stood on the other side of the table, his face blurry from the roiling heat haze coming off the felt. He was holding a knife. "You think I don't know whose table this is?"

Hoyt shook Lars off. Lars's hand came away slathered in blood.

He wiped his hand on his jeans, looking over the table, but didn't see a stray droplet of blood on the burnished wood. He couldn't even see the scars or the scratches and drink rings.

The lurid glow of the deep crimson felt bathed Vickers's flabby face as he drew the knife across his palm, cutting it deeply. He made a cup of his hand, brimming with blood. "I know this was Skip Skibski's custom job," he said. Lars backed away from it, seeing it with new eyes.

Lars's dad used to trade the Skibski story as they shot 8-ball at the Flea Market Tavern, the only place in town that let drunks bring their kids in with them. The last of the dirty pool hall sharks to make it big, Skibski won the nationals four years running before he lost to Lou Henenlotter.

Skibski was a short man, almost a dwarf, and ranted to anyone who'd listen that he would've won on a shorter table. He had this special tournament table made, sparing no expense——imported limestone slate from Mexico, mahogany wood and ivory from the last Pacific whale taken by American boats off the coast of Baja. It was a rigorously crafted tournament table except for its height. He challenged Lou Henenlotter to a private tourney to settle the question, and Henenlotter, a hulking 6'6" Minneapolis bohunk with nothing to prove, eventually knuckled under to accept the challenge.

The story of the game itself was a set-up for every conceivable variety of trick shot, and so changed every time Dad told it, but the end was always the same. Skibski ran Harlem Globetrotter circles around Henenlotter, who couldn't sink anything but the cue ball at first but somehow muscled through and came out ahead. Down two balls and stuck with a shitty lay behind a wall of Big Lou's balls, Skibski took a break to powder his nose. He came back pale and sickly, but he made the shot and the next and the next, though each one looked to take ten years off his life. He sank the 8 and shook Henenlotter's hand, then doubled over and dropped dead.

The coroner found Skibski suffered from cirrhosis, emphysema, an enlarged heart with arteries kinked and clogged like old radiator hoses, and six stab wounds to the belly. The question of who killed Skip Skibski in his own home during a private game with no official significance was their JFK assassination, but nobody ever solved it, because they didn't want it solved. In pool, the balls always went where the careful, patient player put them . . . mostly.

"I heard the stories, too," Vickers said. "I didn't believe 'em, but you made a believer out of me." Squeezing a half pint of blood out of his fist to drizzle into the nearest corner pocket, he grasped his cue with the wounded hand and ran it down the shaft, slicking the glossy wood. "I know what it wants, too. So let's cut the shit, shall we, and fucking *play*."

Vickers leaned on the table and off-handedly jabbed the cue ball. It rolled with a weird, slow inevitability over to nick the 3, transferring all its momentum to the bright scarlet ball, which rolled headwards as if pushed by an invisible hand to kiss the 9 and nudge it, ever so gently, into the side pocket.

Vickers stood tall and looked across the table at Hoyt. His southpaw palm and both forearms smoked where his wiry hair had been singed away, and blisters were already forming where he'd touched the table. The room reeked of burnt hair and melted pennies.

"Rack 'em up," he said, but Sonny and his friend shared a significant, beetle-browed stare and got the fuck out of there. "You're both fired," Vickers shouted at their backs, but he didn't seem to care all that much. Sheathing the knife on his belt, he picked up his beer and pointed at Lars.

Lars burned his hands racking up the balls. Hoyt chuckled when he saw Lars blowing on his palms. "You've got to burn," he said, "in order to shine."

Hoyt broke, sinking the 4 and the 8, which chased each other to the corner pocket like two piglets going for a single teat. He tried to combo the 1 on the 9, but it caromed off without moving the ultimate ball at all. 9 just spun on its axis in place, an immovable object.

Vickers squeezed his fist, but barely a drop came out. It looked withered and infected, a crabbed claw that barely opened to hold the cue. Nonetheless, Vickers finger-painted FUCK YOU on the gleaming mahogany bumper, called his pocket with a dip of his cue, and methodically sank the 1, the 2 and the 3, all in the same pocket; but as Vickers set his sights on the 5 and took his shot, Hoyt spat blood all over the table.

He'd bitten right through his tongue and pursed his lips like blowing a trumpet, so a fine mist of syrupy red saliva settled over the moving balls. It hissed like butter on a skillet, wherever it touched the blood-engorged felt.

Vickers cried foul, punched himself full in the face and blew bloody snot on the table to change the outcome, but to no avail. The 5 waddled away drunkenly, rebounding off the far rail to drop into the wrong pocket.

Vickers raged at Lars, but what could he do? What were the rules of this game? When were there ever any rules?

"Pull it," Hoyt snarled.

"Leave it alone." Vickers drew his knife.

Lars went over to the pocket and looked down there, expecting to see anything but a ball. Reaching into it felt like sticking your hand in a rattlesnake nest. The ball was so hot, his fingers wouldn't clasp it, but he wrapped his fist in the tail of his flannel shirt and drew it out. The ball dropped and bounced across the table, coming to rest on the head point as if dragged by a magnet.

Lars looked from the table to the players and understood, at last, one little mystery. Skibski stabbed himself to win the game, to feed the table or whatever lived inside it. He had to figure his dad and all his friends, killing themselves for the meaningless game with every drink, smoke and missed night of sleep, knew it too, but couldn't come out and say it. That which is understood need not be discussed . . .

Hoyt leaned over the table like a condemned man looking over his last meal. Vickers stood across from him, bellowing, "Stupid little prick, I was bleeding for this game before you were born . . . "

Hoyt sank the 5.

"I shit bigger than you, you candy-ass tweaker cheat . . . "

Hoyt sank the 6.

"I'll fucking *end* you! You ain't got enough blood to take me . . . "

Hoyt sank the 7.

"You're dead, d'you hear me, boy? *Dead* . . . "

Hoyt sank the 8.

"I will crack you open and eat your beating heart before your dying eyes . . . "

Hoyt lifted his cue and pointed it at Vickers's face as if he was going to say something clever, then just smiled and bent to take his shot.

"This game don't mean shit . . . This table ain't shit . . . *You* ain't shit . . . "

Hoyt shot without notching the cue. The stick shredded the red felt, making a long grinning rip.

The cue ball rocketed into the 9 with a wicked backspin, sending it flying off the table and into Vickers's face, where it seemed to vanish.

Vickers rocked back on his heels, clutching his throat. His jaw worked, trying to get another word out, but it was stopped up with the 9, which peeked out between his shattered teeth. A one in a million shot, it had somehow forced its way in at the peak of Vickers's tantrum, but now could not be expelled. Vickers pounded on the table, gobs of bloody snot spraying from his blocked nostrils. Hoyt watched until Vickers stumbled and slumped across the table. His face began to sizzle and lazy tongues of flame licked up from his thinning hair.

The table simmered. Where the felt was ripped, Lars could see a patch of naked slate, worm-eaten and gnarled with Aztec hieroglyphs or some shit, the grooves and pits filled with maroon crumbs of dried blood like a field of flea droppings, but all this burned away as the slate began to glow like lava.

No way it was just an ordinary stone, and looking at it, Lars's head crawled with indescribable pictures, like it wanted to be known and worshipped. Like it was one of those altars on which they chopped the beating hearts out of a hundred men at a throw to feed their greedy gods, and maybe there was nobody up there waiting for their banquet of hearts, but maybe that stone got so glutted with blood that it became a kind of god, itself, and maybe a sawed-off pool shark heard about that terrible stone, and saw an angle.

The whole table flexed and subsided, surged and shuddered. It was breathing.

"Jump Around" blasted from the unplugged jukebox, making Lars jump.

Hoyt let his stick fall to the floor and turned to Lars. "I win. Give me my prize."

Lars held his hands up in surrender, approaching the table like it was the last place he wanted to go. "You win," he said, and reaching for his pocket, he kicked the bricks supporting the nearest leg of the table.

Two of his toes cracked inside his steel-toed boot. The lopsided table crashed to the floor with a deafening bang like a cargo container falling from a great height, and a crack shot through the slate like lightning. Live steam gushed out of the fissure, the sound like a long, hissing sob.

The glow of it guttered and dimmed, but now the same awful light poured out of Hoyt's eyes like the vapor of burning blood. His bloody forked tongue lolled out of his mouth when he uttered Lars's name.

Lars looked around and took up the only protection he could find. Snatching a cue off the wall, he held it up like a baseball bat, but Hoyt easily swatted away his tentative swings and kept coming.

Always, when he was forced to play, Lars worked the pockets capably enough until the final ball, and no matter how he tried to unfuck his head, he involuntarily flinched when he took the shot, scratched and lost.

Hoyt didn't give him a chance to flinch. Stepping into the kid's path, Lars thrust the cue like a spear and hit him dead in his left eye.

The cue stick crushed the eye like an olive and hit a bony resistance at the back of the optic cavity. Hoyt lurched as if he'd just bumped into someone, then shoved himself forward against the stabbing stick. Lars felt with hideous intimacy the back wall of the eye socket collapse, the cue sinking into the vault of Hoyt's brain. Hoyt took a halting step, then another, Lars adjusting his grip as the cue sank deeper into Hoyt's skull, growing ever shorter as Hoyt drew closer.

Hoyt jerked to a stop as the cue bumped into something else, that could only be the back of his skull. Hoyt reached out, his clawed fingers pawing at Lars's chest, looking for his money . . . or his heart. Molten red light gushed out of his mouth.

Lars twisted the butt of the cue to the right, whipping Hoyt's head sideways on his neck. Reaching around his spasming bulk, Lars grasped the slimy end of the cue that had passed entirely through Hoyt's skull and whipped it around as hard as he could with both hands.

It was so easy in the movies, like breaking a breadstick, but the real thing was more like uprooting a green sapling. Lars nearly threw his shoulder out whipping Hoyt's head around until it looked down at its own skinny ass. Finally, Hoyt's neck snapped and he dropped to the floor as if poleaxed.

Vickers was a dying bonfire, roiling smoke and crackling fat. Steam continued to pour out of the fatal fault in the slate, dousing the lamp and raining condensation that sizzled and turned back to steam.

Lars turned to leave, but he felt such an urgent heat in his chest that he thought for a second he was having a heart attack. That figures, he thought, for what else could a heart do, that had witnessed what he'd seen?

His hand went to his chest and he realized what it was. Taking out Vickers's wad of cash, he threw it on the table, then Hoyt's roll. He thought for a moment about taking the $50 he was owed and certainly had earned, but the money was already smoldering ash.

Lars kicked the jukebox over on its side, then headed for the exit of Ringo's Pool Room, but he looked outside before he opened the door, and stopped.

A cop was parked next to his El Camino, lights splashing cobalt and crimson, running Lars's plate and sipping his coffee. He could go out there and get in his car like any solid citizen, but he was drenched in tacky blood from collar to combat boots. He'd be lucky to just get arrested, lucky not to be executed on the spot.

He started to turn to go find the back door when a hand fell on his shoulder. "How about a game of cutthroat?"

Lars couldn't bring himself to look at Hoyt or Vickers, but he looked one last time at the cop, weighing the angles and risks of the two games. One he might suck at, but the other, nobody like him could win.

"Rack 'em up," he said.

Cody Goodfellow has written eight novels and five collections. He wrote, co-produced and scored the notorious Lovecraftian hygiene films Baby Got Bass *and* Stay At Home Dad, *which can be viewed on YouTube, and presides over several Cthulhu Prayer Breakfasts each year.*

SOMETHING SINISTER IS HIDING IN THE SMALL TOWN OF PERCY, INDIANA...
TOUCH THE NIGHT
MAX BOOTH III

ANTIOCH
Jessica Leonard

And now, an excerpt from Jessica Leonard's *Antioch*, out now from Perpetual Motion Machine

BESS JACKSON LIVED in a small two-bedroom home with an open floorplan and an attached garage, which she'd originally purchased with a man. But that man wasn't around anymore. Which is, in more ways than one, how she found herself arriving home at night in a car belonging to someone entirely different. This new man was named Greg, and while he wasn't the first person she'd dated since she'd found herself the sole owner of her home, it still, years later, felt odd to be in this place with someone else.

"Should I walk you in?" Greg asked.

"You don't need to do that," Bess replied. The neighborhood was well-lit with houses that were a little too close to each other.

"Yeah, but maybe I should. I mean, you never know in Antioch. Vlad could be hiding in your coat closet. I'd better come in. Just to make sure you're safe."

Bess rolled her eyes and laughed; it was all a fun joke. But there was enough truth behind the joke to make her accept the offer. The Impaler Murders began in Antioch nearly two years ago, and as brave as Bess liked to think she was, it made living alone a little more ominous sometimes. Two years was a long time to be afraid. It made a person weary.

Once inside, Greg made a show of looking under her couch for any murderers. Before she could stop him, he poked his head into the garage and called out to potential serial killers. But his joke—which was already stretched thin—seemed to snap entirely when he saw the garage.

"What's all this?" he asked.

"All this" was the overstatement of the year. Inside the garage there was only a lone card table, its top decorated with swipes of dust, a spiral bound notebook, and a pristine shortwave radio.

"That," Bess said with pride, "is my shortwave, a Grundig Satellit 750." She gazed lovingly at her radio, then at Greg with somewhat less admiration.

"What's it do?" Greg said, less a formal question and more of a "Why am I looking at a radio?" rhetorical.

As far as first dates went, this was not Bess's worst. Greg was handsome enough, although his precisely gelled blond hair and ample use of Axe body spray wasn't something Bess usually looked for in a man. He'd been mostly polite to her and while he didn't seem interested in her as a person, he had enough manners to try and fake it.

"It just, you know, listens. It searches." Shortwave as a hobby wasn't something easily explained. She wished he hadn't seen the radio. Having her head impaled on a stick now seemed at least somewhat less exhausting than continuing a conversation with someone too polite to say they didn't care.

"Huh," Greg said, looking around at the empty white walls. The room had the musty smell of a dirt-floored cellar. She could tell he was sorry he'd offered to walk her in. He certainly hadn't foreseen hanging out in a gross, empty garage looking at a radio. "Have you been doing this long?"

"Since I was fifteen. My dad got me my first radio."

"Was it something you picked up from him?" Greg asked, and Bess heard the hope in his voice. Maybe it was a family thing. His family was into tennis, and perhaps her family preferred little radios.

"No," Bess said, her eyes on the floor, for some reason sorry to be disappointing him. "I had this Amelia Earhart obsession. That really got me going."

"Did she use one of these?"

"No, well, I mean, yeah, I guess maybe. But that wasn't it. Do you know much about her?"

"Earhart? She was a pilot who crashed. That's pretty much all my knowledge on the subject."

"Yeah, and that's basically it, but her disappearance is still a huge mystery. There are tons of theories about what happened to her. Some think she crashed into the ocean, but there are other people who think different." She glanced back at the radio, trying to decide how to continue. The more rational part of her brain told her not to continue at all. But goddammit, once she got on a roll about Earhart theories she couldn't help herself. A big part of her wanted to tell him everything even if he didn't care. He wasn't going to stop her, and it was so rare to have a captive audience. "So, one of the theories says a girl heard transmissions from Amelia Earhart the night she went missing. She heard them on her shortwave radio, but no one believed her. She reported it to the coast guard back then, but they dismissed it right away. So that's kind of how it started for me. Learning about those transmissions."

"It's a conspiracy theory."

"I guess. But no one can for sure prove or disprove it."

"That's what a conspiracy theory is," Greg said.

"Okay, well, a conspiracy theory shaped my life."

Greg shrugged. "It happens." He stuck his hands in his pockets and walked to the radio. He pointed to a small glass ashtray sitting next to it. "Oh hey, fantastic. Do you mind if I . . . "

"Knock yourself out," Bess said. It was the first time he'd alluded to being a smoker all night, and Bess wondered if this hidden vice accounted for all the Axe Body Spray.

Greg lit a cigarette from a pack he had hidden inside the inner pocket of his sports jacket and then tucked them away without offering one. "Tell me more. What does this girl hear on the radio?"

"She hears a lot of stuff. Things which later lead some people to think Amelia actually landed her plane off Gardner Island, but died there before she could be located or rescued."

"I've never heard of Gardner Island."

"It's called Nikumaroro now."

"I've heard of that even less." Greg took a long draw from his cigarette and exhaled away from Bess and the radio. Ever polite. "But I want to know the conspiracy. Give me the weird shit. You didn't get obsessed with radios for no reason. Not just because some girl said she maybe heard something neat once."

Bess tried to think of an easy way to tell the story. Every detail of Betty's notebook and the interpretations of what she claimed to hear was etched into Bess's brain, but how much of it was actually interesting? And why was she still interested in being interesting? She didn't have any real desire to ever see Greg again, but here she was, choosing her words carefully and trying to impress. Maybe she was polite too.

"Okay, so this girl, her name's Betty, she hears a transmission while she's cruising around on the shortwave and the voice says, 'This is Amelia Earhart.' And Betty always keeps a notebook with her while she's messing with the radio because you never know what you might hear and sometimes she wrote down song lyrics and stuff because she was fifteen and that's what kids do, I guess." Bess paused for breath and looked at Greg, who was smiling at her like she was adorable—not in an attractive way, more like in a pitying way. She forged ahead. "So she writes down everything she hears and when some people who knew a thing or two actually got ahold of the notebook a few decades later, and read the things she said, some of it started to make sense. And it led some people to Gardner."

"What parts made sense?"

"She wrote down 'N.Y.' a few times, which she later said was an abbreviation for New York City. Like, Earhart kept repeating New York City. Which doesn't make any sense. Except it does when you think about how Gardner is a coral atoll and right there along it is the wreck of the SS Norwich City. Norwich City was a steamer that ran aground there in 1929. The wreck was a hazard, everyone knew about it. If she could see it and she was trying to tell people where she was, it makes sense that maybe she was saying the name of the ship. Not New York City, but Norwich City. You see?"

"That's actually really interesting." Greg sounded impressed or surprised, Bess couldn't decide which. "Is there more?"

"There is, but it can take forever to really get into it, and I'm pretty tired." She gave the sheepish smile of the person who admits they're sleepy first. She'd purposely set their first date for a Wednesday night so she could easily use the excuse of getting to bed early for work the next day.

"Oh yeah, of course." He squashed out his cigarette in the ashtray. "I didn't mean to keep you up. Thanks for a nice night, Bess." Greg leaned in and kissed her on the cheek. He pointed to the table. "Is that notebook like Betty's?" He was gesturing to a small green notebook with a cheap ink pen Bess stole from a motel lying across it.

"Oh, gosh. Yeah, I guess it is. I like to write down stuff sometimes. When I can't sleep at night it helps me relax. I guess because it's basically mindless. It's like meditating. Instead of chanting or whatever, I write."

Greg smiled. "That's nice. I like that idea. I'll call you later, okay?"

Bess was positive this was a lie. "Should I walk you back out now?

You know, the Impaler . . . woooo," she made a low key ghost noise and wiggled her fingers ominously.

"Nah—I'm safe as safe can be, Bess. You know old Vlad only likes the ladies." Greg laughed. Bess gave a little smile to show she was a good sport, too well-mannered to let on that his comment unnerved her. She had never known a single one of Vlad the Impaler's six victims, but sometimes she had nightmares about them. In her dreams the six heads sat on her kitchen counter, all talking at once. Sometimes they spoke in different languages. Sometimes they made screeching noises so loud Bess would have to cover her ears. As she tried to decipher what they were telling her, a large shadow would appear in the doorway. The heads would fall silent. She could never understand what they were saying.

Once Greg's car had pulled away from her house, Bess changed into blue pajama pants and an old white tee shirt. There was a full six pack of Fat Tire waiting in the fridge. She opened one with the tulip-shaped bottle opener that hung from her wall and took a few swallows before retreating to the worn charcoal grey couch and turning on the television. She flipped through the channels too quickly to register what was on any of them, then scrolled through again, slower this time, trying to pay attention.

Bess stopped on the local news. She thought back to Greg telling her he'd better walk her in so Vlad didn't get her. There hadn't been a new victim in months. She didn't know if she would be more relieved to hear nothing on the news, or to hear they'd found his next victim—head spiked onto a PVC pipe in some abandoned lot in Antioch, body never to be found. If they found someone else she could feel safe for a couple of months.

Bess shook her head and changed the channel, lingering on an old episode of *MythBusters* before giving up and switching it off entirely. Restless energy twitched through her limbs. The beer was on her coffee table and she plucked it up and gulped some down before replacing it and closing her eyes, allowing her mind to wander.

The repetitive caw of seagulls filled her ears. Bess pictured Amelia Earhart out there in the ocean with her injured navigator, Fred Noonan. Fred slipping in and out of lucidity, yelling for his wife and trying to run out of the plane and into the ocean. The rising tide lapping into the Lockheed Electra. She smelled the salt air and saw the black profile of the Norwich City like a hole punched into an already dark sky.

"This is Amelia Earhart."

Frantic SOS signals sent out to possibly no one. Everything had gone so wrong and now her legacy would sink into this one tragic failure.

Where would she have gone? Bess wondered if she drowned straight away—her legs scraped and cut by jagged bits of coral, her muscles too exhausted to carry her to shore—or if she made it to the beach before dying of exposure, starvation, or dehydration. Giant coconut crabs would carry away her body bit by bit. The ocean would overtake her plane. Her existence would be erased.

Bess played each scenario out in her mind. Sometimes Noonan was with her, sometimes not. Sometimes she watched him drown as he raved and fought against the ocean.

Her eyes popped open. Her body was damp with sweat. She'd fallen asleep. At first she thought she'd been dreaming about Vlad but then it came back to her.

Amelia.

After Earhart's disappearance, rumors started to spread that she'd been captured by the Japanese. At the time, any English-speaking women broadcasting Japanese propaganda were known as "Tokyo Rose", and some theorized one of the women on the radio might be Earhart. Her husband, George Putnam, investigated these rumors diligently. He listened to hours of recordings, but he never heard his wife's voice.

Bess breathed deep and reached for her beer. It was warm and a little flat, but Bess gulped it down as fast as she could. She stood and tried to stretch out the kink that had settled into her shoulders. For a second, she considered going to bed but knew she would never get back to sleep.

The garage always felt a little too warm for most people, but Bess thought the temperature was perfect. Dragging a folding chair over from the corner of the room, she settled herself at the card table. She clicked the radio on and slowly scanned through the channels, pausing here and there, moving backward, trying to pick up a strong signal.

With a meticulous hand she wrote the date at the top of a fresh page in her notebook. Jotting down bits and pieces she found interesting as she went, Bess began her nightly meditation. She switched between the upper and lower sideband setting to hear random voice communications. Sometimes she would linger over the beep-screeches of data signals, letting the noise overtake her, thinking about how it was so senseless to the ear—to someone who didn't know better—but with the right programs it could be translated. The noises were her religious chants. She wrote down weather conditions being broadcast to pilots over the ocean, collected international news reports alongside song lyrics.

She closed her eyes and listened in awe to the foreign language broadcasts, the words like a prayer she couldn't quite understand but found comfort in. From time to time she listened in on truckers and ham radio operators talking back and forth. She especially liked hearing people use Morse code. It was something she learned in her early twenties, and while she missed some things, she'd learned enough universal abbreviations that she could catch the drift of the secrets people were sharing. Women were referred to as "YL", meaning Young Lady, and men were "OM", Old Man—this was an old language, a gallant one. 88 meant "love and kisses".

Then there was the Buzzer. Tonight seemed like a Buzzer kind of night. Bess tuned her receiver to frequency 4625 kHz. A dull endless hum filled the garage. It was legendary in the shortwave world, a Russian station that had been playing this same monotonous tone since the early 80's, occasionally joined by a low deep foghorn-like sound. Maybe once a week there would be a word or two in Russian.

After about an hour of buzzing her nerves were calm and her mind was easy. Her eyelids began to droop but she didn't want to leave the radio. To go into the quiet house would be to give her imagination free reign once again. The station drowned out her dreams.

This is Amelia Earhart
This is Amelia Earhart

Bess jerked awake. A page of her notebook was stuck to her cheek and came up with her head before gravity caught on to what was happening and yanked the book back to the table.

SOS
SOS

Bess observed the radio, unsure if the transmissions were real or following her out of her dreams.

I can feel it

It wasn't a dream. Someone was broadcasting an SOS message across the shortwave frequencies. Quickly, Bess snatched up her pen and scribbled down the last line of the message and waited.

Intel

Intel? Was this some sort of military broadcast? Those were usually encrypted. Much of the modern world had moved on from the shortwave for sensitive communications, but if this was a true distress call there was no telling who it may or may not be.

Intel here

At this point a second voice rang out, farther away but loud.

Margaret! Margaret!

Chills ran through Bess's body. There was a pause before the first voice resumed. The words were garbled, the beginnings being cut off or lost completely. The signal was weak, but Bess was afraid to adjust the radio for fear of losing it altogether.

. . . since feast day
It's rising now
Bevington
Bevington
. . . find buddy

Bess wrote as fast as she could, desperately trying to get down as much of the message as possible.

SOS
SOS
Can you hear?

The second voice once again called for Margaret. But then something else. It sounded like the word "dragging." From far away she heard a man yelling to Margaret about dragging something. Or that something was dragging. Maybe Margaret was dragging. It was too hard to make out.

Intel here

The original woman spoke again, this time in a hushed tone like a stage whisper.

Tell her
Tell her
Tell Her

There was another long pause. Either the transmission ended or the signal was entirely lost. She laid down her pen and stared at it, hearing only static. And then:

This is Amelia Earhart

The clicky buzz-hum of radio static hung heavy in the muggy, unairconditioned garage. Bess breathed deep through her mouth and let the late August humidity coat the inside of her throat. She looked down at her notebook. Her chicken scratch shorthand looked back at her. Capital E, squiggle line, lowercase t.

She continued with the deep, slow breaths until her heart slowed from a thud to an insistent knock. Reaching with measured, deliberate motions, Bess clicked off her radio. The longer she examined what she'd written, the more obvious it became—someone was fucking with her.

"Very funny," she said to no one, or maybe the room.

Someone wanted to play a trick on her.

"But how did they know what frequency I'd be on?"

The room did not answer, but rather presented her with more questions.

Who would play a trick on you? Who would care enough? No one knows you.

"I guess Greg knew about the Earhart stuff."

Only what you told him.

"Even Carrie White got pranked."

Carrie was more popular than you.

"I'm a fucking adult. I don't need to be popular."

The room did not answer, but instead kept a sort of smug silence. Its point had been made. This transmission probably wasn't directed at Bess.

But that didn't mean it wasn't a hoax, it was just one being played on someone else. Bess hearing it was like when someone in a crowd waves at someone behind you. And you *think* they're waving at you, so you wave back . . .

If it was a prank, why wouldn't they recite the real Earhart transmission? Betty's notebook pages detailing the possible last transmissions of Earhart are online—scanned and transcribed with annotations—for the world to see. So what would be the purpose of altering the message? Unless that repeated line, "Intel," meant this was some sort of code.

Anyone acquainted with Earhart theories would catch some familiar phrases in there. Like "Bevington." Eric Bevington was a Cadet Officer at the British Gilbert and Ellice Islands Colony. Three months after Earhart disappeared, he snapped an infamous photo just off the west end of Gardner Island. Some claim to see signs of what might be the landing gear of a Lockheed Electra poking out above the water. The black, burnt-out remains of the SS Norwich City lolls in the background. Bevington and his photo fit into the Earhart mythos, but not into her transmissions.

"Unless it was a ghost," Bess said, trying out the words to see how they sounded. The notion that Amelia Earhart's ghost had reached out to her through a shortwave radio seemed at least somewhat unlikely.

She looked at the notebook. The SOS was undeniable. Someone needed help. Someone named Amelia Earhart. Or possibly Margaret. And there it was again. Like Bevington, Margaret was close, but not quite right.

In Betty's notebook, where she transcribed what she believed to be transmissions from Earhart, there are several references to a man—presumably navigator Fred Noonan—shouting the name Marie over and over. Which doesn't mean anything until you take a minute to consider that Noonan's wife was named Mary Bea, and then you have to wonder. Marie. Mary Bea. New York City. Norwich City.

Not Margaret.

But *close*.

Bess thrust her thin fingers into her dark mass of curly hair and massaged the sides of her head. There was no clock in the garage but she knew it must be early morning. Her knees cracked when she stood. The bright white notebook paper glared up at her. She turned her back on it.

Inside the house proper, Bess trudged down her short hallway and into the bedroom. The floor was spattered with dirty clothes and shoes— a dropping off station rather than a lived-in space. She flopped diagonally across the bed and was asleep within minutes, sinking into the hard, dreamless sleep of the dead.

READ THE REST IN JESSICA LEONARD'S *ANTIOCH*, AVAILABLE NOW!

CPSIA information can be obtained
at www.ICGtesting.com
Printed in the USA
LVHW090655221120
672145LV00018B/231